W9-CGO-706

*"Blow me again."*

Meg's startled gaze flew to where Nick sat on the bed, grinning wickedly at her. She drew in a much-needed breath, trying to calm her racing nerves. Instead, her blood raced as graphic images— *enticing possibilities*—began tumbling through her mind. And she might as well start by giving Nick what he asked for. Lowering her head, she blew lightly on his arm.

"Damn. It feels all hot and tingly. What did you call this stuff?"

"Shiver Cream. You like it?" Meg teased, turning to place the container back on the bedside table.

"Yeah," he said softly. "Did you give it a good review?"

Meg blew lightly on his wrist a second time. "What do you think?"

Nick's eyes widened and he shuddered. "I think it's incredible," he said with a groan. His sinful and slightly mischievous gaze captured hers. "Want me to do you?"

A vision of those gorgeous lips hovering over her flesh gripped her, made her breasts go heavy, her nipples bud. She ached for him. "Yes," Meg finally squeaked. *"Definitely, yes."*

# Blaze™

Dear Reader,

If you like a little giggle with your sizzle, then this might be the book for you. Personally, I am utterly thrilled to be writing for Blaze. This bold, innovative new line provides such scope for the imagination and is the perfect forum for contemporary characters prone to a little scandalous behavior. What fun! It's a writer's dream.

Set in Atlanta amid a weeklong sex-toy trade show, *Just Toying Around...* is long on laughs and even longer on steamy sensuality. Meg Sugarbaker is a pastry chef who moonlights as the online sex-toy critic, Desiree Moon. Trouble is, Meg's true sexual experiences can be counted on her pinky finger and, sadly, lasted about as long as it takes to nuke a bag of microwave popcorn. Attorney Nick Devereau suspects Desiree's secret, and is determined to declare her a fraud. But as the week progresses, Nick becomes less interested in uncovering the truth and more interested in uncovering *her*.

I hope you enjoy reading about Meg and Nick's wicked games....

Enjoy,

*Rhonda Nelson*

P.S. Be sure to look for my next Blaze book, *Show & Tell*, available in April 2003!

# JUST TOYING AROUND...

*Rhonda Nelson*

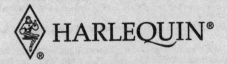

HARLEQUIN®

TORONTO • NEW YORK • LONDON
AMSTERDAM • PARIS • SYDNEY • HAMBURG
STOCKHOLM • ATHENS • TOKYO • MILAN • MADRID
PRAGUE • WARSAW • BUDAPEST • AUCKLAND

If you purchased this book without a cover you should be aware
that this book is stolen property. It was reported as "unsold and
destroyed" to the publisher, and neither the author nor the
publisher has received any payment for this "stripped book."

If you're lucky, at some point in your life
you'll find a true friend of the heart, someone who laughs with you,
cries with you and always believes in you. And if you're truly
blessed, you'll be able to call that person your sister.
This book is dedicated to Brooke Vanderford,
my very own *friendster*.
I love you, Froggy. This one is yours.

ISBN 0-373-79079-1

JUST TOYING AROUND...

Copyright © 2003 by Rhonda Nelson.

All rights reserved. Except for use in any review, the reproduction or
utilization of this work in whole or in part in any form by any electronic,
mechanical or other means, now known or hereafter invented, including
xerography, photocopying and recording, or in any information storage
or retrieval system, is forbidden without the written permission of the
publisher, Harlequin Enterprises Limited, 225 Duncan Mill Road,
Don Mills, Ontario, Canada M3B 3K9.

All characters in this book have no existence outside the imagination of
the author and have no relation whatsoever to anyone bearing the same
name or names. They are not even distantly inspired by any individual
known or unknown to the author, and all incidents are pure invention.

This edition published by arrangement with Harlequin Books S.A.

® and TM are trademarks of the publisher. Trademarks indicated with
® are registered in the United States Patent and Trademark Office, the
Canadian Trade Marks Office and in other countries.

Visit us at www.eHarlequin.com

**Printed in U.S.A.**

# 1

"ARE YOU SURE THAT'S HER?"

"Yes, that's her," Nick Devereau's brother, Ron, hissed impatiently. "What do you take me for? An idiot?"

Ninety-nine percent of the time, yes, Nick thought with a beleaguered sigh. There were times when being the responsible son was really inconvenient. Like now.

"I've done my homework on this one," Ron insisted. "That's definitely Desiree Moon."

"If you'd done your homework," Nick retorted tightly, "you'd know her real name by now."

Which would have made Nick's work considerably easier. He could have simply threatened her with a libel suit, instead of resorting to tactics so beneath him it made his gut clench with dread. Nick had foisted his substantial caseload off onto his partner, had essentially put his entire life on hold in order to handle another Ron crisis. Honestly, would he never shrug this albatross off his neck? Would he always wear an armor of guilt beneath the hard-earned suit of his success?

How on earth had he let Ron talk him into this ill-conceived plan? he wondered again. Nick mentally snorted. Hell, he hadn't been talked into anything. He'd been blackmailed. Threatened. Coerced. Sent on the you-were-Dad's-favorite Guilt Express, a one-way ticket to the land of self-reproof. It didn't matter that Nick was blameless, that he hadn't been responsible for his father's unfair favoritism. It only mattered that it was true. And therein lay the rub.

Forcing the somber thoughts away, Nick shifted in the comfortable hotel chair and continued to pretend to read the paper while he covertly studied his prey.

Desiree Moon.

The infamous online sex-toy critic.

The woman Ron had asked him to seduce. Nick had flatly refused, of course. Honestly. He'd be damned before he'd become Ron's whore. But he had agreed to spy on her, charm her, to see if he could discover any information Ron might use against her to save his business.

Thank God she wasn't the pock-faced-three-hundred pound-mustached-hag-standing-at-the-ironing-board-wearing-a-muumuu nightmare his overactive imagination had tortured him with over the past week.

As a corporate attorney Nick had learned how to finesse both genders, learned how to study body language and pinpoint weaknesses, vanities. The art of flirtation was also a handy tool and Nick had mastered it over the years. Still, if she'd been the nightmare his sadistic imagination had recently plagued him with, Nick would have been hard pressed to pull off this charade. He was good, but not that good.

Nick's lips twisted into a wry grin. His conscience had devised a peculiar punishment—penance, he supposed—for agreeing to do something so underhanded. As soon as he'd committed himself to helping Ron, it had staged a rebellion in his dreams, had tantalized him with visions of himself and a voluptuous goddess in the throes of acts so carnal, so depraved that Nick could scarcely believe they could be borne of his own imagination. Then, in the dream, just as he lay poised on the brink of the ultimate, most mind-blowing orgasm...she'd change—into the hag.

It was horrid.

And all he deserved, given what he'd agreed to do.

Regrettably, he'd been left with little choice. In addition to sending him on another lengthy guilt trip, Ron had played the *Mother* card, and Nick would do whatever he had to in order to protect his mother. Nick wasn't the only one Ron could play and, though Nick had tried for years, he still hadn't been able to get his mother to protect her retirement funds, shelter them out of Ron's reach. If she couldn't earn absolution for her husband's shortcomings, she'd buy it. Nick sighed. He couldn't let her do it again. It was that simple, and that complicated.

Furthermore, after Ron's last so-called loan—a substantial sum Nick had never seen a penny of returned—Nick had vowed not to lend him any more money. He would help Ron any other way he could, but the days of simply handing money over to him to help assuage his own guilt for being the favorite son were a thing of the past. It hadn't been his fault that their father had showered Nick with attention and praise and that Ron had essentially been a forgotten child. No, not forgotten, Nick realized. More like ignored. But no matter how many times Nick tried to tell himself that his father's partiality wasn't his fault, there still remained a little part of him that couldn't be convinced, that held on to the guilt.

So here he sat in the hotel lobby of one of Atlanta's premiere hotels to attend a sex-toy trade show and charm Desiree Moon, the Howard Stern of the online sex-toy world. The woman who, with her acid-tongued reviews of Ron's products, had slowly but surely run his brother's first semi-lucrative business into the ground. The only way to save the business was to discredit her as a critic. For reasons which escaped Nick, Ron suspected her of being a fraud, of lying about her expertise.

That's where Nick came in. He would spy on her, gather the necessary information to prove Ron's theory, and Ron would out her to the adult-toy world. Ron's business would rebound, thus—since Nick had absolutely refused to bail him out of another deal gone sour—Ron wouldn't approach their mother for help.

Though pride would never allow Abigail Devereau to admit it, her funds were in serious trouble from previous Ron-bail-outs and they simply couldn't withstand another handout of this magnitude. Nick knew that she'd do it anyway. She always had. That had been her way of dealing with their father's lack of attention to his youngest son. His mother had overcompensated, showering Ron with love, with gifts, with whatever she could in order to fill the void of his father's inattention. Sadly, the money would be gone before she'd run out of guilt.

So Nick had stepped in to prevent that from happening—he owed his mother too much. Though she wouldn't allow him to manage her funds—the result of Ron's interference—he still couldn't permit her to essentially commit financial suicide.

Nick wasn't absolutely certain that Ron would go to their mother, but the threat had been enough to keep Nick from calling Ron's bluff. Had been enough to propel Nick to help him. Furthermore, though he didn't always understand him, Nick loved Ron and longed for a closer relationship with him.

Besides, there was something distinctly distasteful about his mother's retirement money being used to produce and market sex toys. It was unnatural.

Just like the damned toys.

Nick suppressed a shudder. Males and females were created with conjoining parts, made to come together in a perfectly natural way. Nick was sure alkaline batteries were never meant to be a part of it.

Besides, any man who couldn't pleasure a woman without the aid of some new-age latex, battery-operated gadget should forget the business altogether and let his pecker petrify from disuse. He'd use his own rod, thank you very much, and if for some reason he left a woman unsatisfied—which had *never* happened—then there were other more creative methods to accomplish the same end.

In Nick's opinion, every man owed it to his partner to become a competent lover. He could personally draw an orgasm from a woman in under ninety seconds. No brag, just fact. And he used his own equipment.

"Hey, she's pretty hot," Ron whispered roughly. "Now you can quit complaining. This should be a walk in the park for you."

Nick scowled. "This is not going to be a walk in the park. It's a deceitful, underhanded course of action that surely could have been avoided with a little—"

"Yeah, yeah. Save your lawyer talk, Nick. She's ruining me," Ron reminded him hotly. "Are you going to help me or not?"

Did he really have a choice? Nick wondered futilely. He sighed. "I said I would."

Ron grunted in response.

Nick snuck another peek at his target. As for her being hot, how could Ron even tell? The woman wore a trench coat, a big floppy hat and sunglasses that would have dwarfed Mike Ditka's big head. Hell, she could be hiding all sorts of imperfections underneath that getup.

The garb nevertheless drew a reluctant grin from Nick. Her blatant attempt at incognito had definitely backfired. Almost every person in the hotel lobby had swiveled a double take at the ridiculous outfit.

Like everyone else in the room, the only part of her anatomy Nick could truly see was her mouth.

And what a mouth.

Ripe, curved to perfection, naturally pink, not globbed up with thick, pasty lipstick and just a fraction over-full. It was the most carnal mouth Nick had ever seen and instantly redeemed whatever imperfections she might or might not have. Kissing her would be a treat.

"She's headed for the elevators," Ron muttered needlessly. "It's show time, big brother. The check-in clerk and I worked out a little deal. Your rooms have connecting doors."

Nick shuddered to think what sort of deal Ron and the hotel employee had "worked out." The connecting door would definitely be a perk, though. He'd be able to monitor her comings and goings and the proximity would work to his advantage. It would be easier to nurture a relationship. Though he hated to admit it, Ron had managed not to completely bungle this.

"Keep me updated," Ron said. "I'm in nine-oh-nine." He paused, looking momentarily sheepish. "Uh…thanks, Nick. You won't regret this. This one is going to work."

Famous last words, Nick thought, hoping that, for his brother's sake, that would be true. Reluctantly, he stood and leisurely strolled to the bank of elevators where Desiree Moon waited. This was it. For better or for worse, he'd agreed to spend the next five days charming everything but the pants off Desiree Moon. Five days with a self-proclaimed professional. A sex-toy critic. Arguably any red-blooded man's fantasy and yet Nick had never dreaded a woman's company more. More, hell. He'd never dreaded it at all.

MEG SUGARBAKER, aka Desiree Moon, depressed the call button for the elevator and silently prayed again that she wouldn't see anyone she knew at this hotel while attending this damned trade show. None of her co-workers at Atlanta's renowned *Chez Renauld's* knew about her other job and she had to keep it that way. Despite her excellent reputation and years of service to her employer, Meg knew that she'd be fired faster than she could say soufflé if the ultra-conservative Renauld ever learned about her second job.

As far as the rest of the world was concerned, she was only a pastry chef. Not a pastry chef who moonlighted as an online sex-toy critic for *Foreplay,* one of the hottest online e-magazines on the World Wide Web.

Meg still couldn't believe that things had escalated to this degree. Six months ago, in the throes of one of her many bouts of unrelieved sexual frustration, she'd gotten cocktailed and gone online in search of a BOB—a Battery Operated Boyfriend.

She'd gotten more than she bargained for.

She'd gotten the BOB and a job.

Though events from that night were still pretty foggy, Meg remembered jokingly applying for a position with *Foreplay* as a critic, vaguely remembered dreaming up the pseudonym Desiree Moon. After that night, she hadn't given it another thought—until her first box of toys arrived with instructions on how to use and critique them, then upload her reviews onto the Web site.

Morbid fascination, blatant curiosity and a woefully neglected, highly motivated libido had propelled her to explore each and every item in the box. She didn't consciously make the decision to start critiquing the toys; she'd just done it. She hadn't been able to resist.

The compensation had turned out to be incredible, and the extra cash would put her that much closer to her lifelong dream of attending Pierre's Culinary Arts School in Paris. She'd been saving for almost two years, but this job with *Foreplay* would make that dream a reality as early as next summer.

But for every perk, there was always a drawback and Meg's had turned out to be a doozy.

For reasons which escaped her, Meg's Desiree Moon persona had reached semistardom on the Internet through her reviews. She knew her neighbors suspected her of having an affair with the deliveryman—she got bombarded with plain-packaged boxes every day. It seemed as though every adult-toy company across America wanted her to critique their product.

Quite frankly, Meg didn't have a clue why.

As with everything else in her life, when she did something she wanted to do it well. This job had been no different. Each time she critiqued a product, she did so to the absolute best of her ability and she was frank. After all, these were sex toys. Mincing words would hardly benefit anyone. Being honest meant speaking plainly. If a toy didn't stimulate her, if it didn't facilitate orgasm, she said so. Likewise, if it made her come, she said that, too.

As for the toys which required a partner...Meg winged it, BS'ed her way through it. She had to because, ironically, other than one sad, completely unsatisfying experience back in college which had lasted a grand total of two minutes—and had cost her a very lucrative scholarship—Meg had no firsthand experience and wasn't inclined to go to the trouble to get any.

The one and only time Meg had dropped her guard and trusted a man enough to sleep with him, he'd bragged about nailing the Ice Queen—her nickname, she'd found out later—to every jerk in possession of a Y chromosome. Including one of the professors who happened to be on the scholarship board. The scholarship Meg had been all but assured, had worked so hard for, was suddenly snatched out of her reach as a result of a morals clause. That momentary lapse in judgment had wrecked the hell out of her five-year plan. It would never happen again.

Meg sighed. The mind was willing, but the flesh was weak, and growing weaker by the day.

To her eternal frustration, Meg had been cursed with

an extremely hyper libido and, sadly, due to the scholarship fiasco, a mistrustful nature. The latter was not conducive to the former.

Which resulted in perpetual sexual frustration.

How she ended up with such a strong sex drive Meg would never know. She was the only child of a set of aging parents whom she'd never seen display any sort of sexual interest in each other. In fact, her parents seemed to be completely asexual and Meg considered it nothing short of a miracle that she even existed. How her mother had ever dragged her father away from the television—which stayed perpetually tuned to a football game—to get the business done, Meg would never know. If she had to guess, Meg imagined she'd most likely been conceived in the recliner, probably during the half-time show.

At any rate, when Meg critiqued the partner-oriented toys, she gleaned information from magazines, co-workers and close friends who were sexually active. Then she'd invented a partner whom she'd dubbed "Antonio" after a popular Latin superstar to complete the ruse. Meg grinned. What the hell. It was her fantasy. She might as well make it real for herself.

If the editors at *Foreplay* ever found out, or heaven forbid, any of the toy companies discovered the true extent of her sexual experience, she'd be ruined as a critic. She'd lose her job. Going to Paris next summer would be out of the question.

Meg shoved the disturbing thought aside, chastising herself for worrying needlessly. Short of her admitting her lack of experience, how could they find her out? They couldn't, Meg assured herself. She had nothing to be concerned about.

Meg simply loved the freedom her online persona gave her. Online she wasn't just plain old single Meg Sugarbaker, twenty-seven-year-old pastry chef, whose life was about as exciting as a pound cake. She was the mysterious Desiree Moon. She was hot. Sexy. People respected her opinion. The power she had was addictive. In that protected forum, she could give voice to some of her most scandalous thoughts. Things she couldn't share with even her closest friends. Things she'd never dream of sharing without complete anonymity.

Meg boarded the elevator, dragging her wheeled garment bag behind her. The doors had almost closed when a large male hand suddenly thrust between them and halted the process.

The body that belonged to the man was proportionate to the hand. The guy was enormous, built on a monumental scale, easily six-six. He was lean like an athlete, yet heavily muscled.

Meg pushed her floppy hat back and craned her head so that she could get a better look at him.

She felt her eyes go wide and her knees go weak. She smothered a moan.

In addition to owning the most devastatingly perfect male form Meg had ever had the pleasure to gaze upon, the guy was gorgeous. Epitomized sexy. To her near slack-jawed amazement, need broadsided her. Her womb flooded with heat and she immediately cast him as the lead in each and every one of her future sex-with-a-complete-stranger fantasies.

Adios Antonio.

Equally bewildered and intrigued by her instantaneous physical attraction to him, Meg continued her rapt perusal.

Pale tawny locks capped his head and she imagined the same golden shade lightly dusted his muscular chest, legs and forearms beneath his fashionable suit. He was lean cheeked, with a hard, uncompromising jaw. His eyes were slumberous, a rich golden brown, almost caramel, with a hint of sin and mischief thrown in for good measure.

He smiled at her, and an endearing dimple winked in his left cheek. She reciprocated the gesture and melted against the wall for support. This man was art in motion, would make Michelangelo's David weep with shame.

"What floor?" he asked.

Who cares? Meg thought. This floor, that floor. The wall, the shower. Didn't matter to her. Until reason returned, she was open to any and all possibilities.

Looking somewhat bemused, he lightly shrugged and pressed a button on the control panel. "I'm on five," he told her.

*What floor?* Feeling ridiculous, Meg squirmed as a blush warmed her cheeks. She cleared her throat, drew her shoulders back and tilted her jaw to its most flattering angle, vainly making a belated attempt to look cool and sophisticated. Which was ridiculous when she looked like the proverbial mobster's widow. What on earth had possessed her to wear this? "I'm, er, on five as well. Here for the trade show?" she ventured. Would that she could be so lucky.

"No." He winked conspiratorially. "But I am here on business."

Damn. It figured. Meg absently chewed her bottom lip and did a quick inspection of his left hand. No ring. No visible shadow of a ring. Probably never married. Which would lead a sensible, less horny woman to conclude he was either A) Possessed of some hideous character flaw. Or B) He was gay. Good-looking professionals such as this did not remain single otherwise. Meg heaved an internal sigh. He was probably gay.

The elevator glided to a smooth stop and the doors opened with a hydraulic whoosh. He allowed her to exit first. Meg murmured a thanks, then said, "Hope you enjoy your stay."

He grinned. "Thanks."

*Hope you enjoy your stay? What was she? The damned concierge?*

Mentally cursing her own stupidity, Meg started down the hall in search of her room. Gay or no, he'd already made this trip even more interesting than it had promised to be. Meg sighed and mentally ticked off what would be required of her during this trade show. She'd meet the editors of *Foreplay* as well as the vendors of the products she critiqued. She'd been asked to give a Q&A workshop. She'd be busy, she realized, totally engrossed in the trade show and probably wouldn't even have time to fantasize about Mr. Perfect from the elevator, much less pursue anything else with him.

Meg battled a wave of regret at the thought, but resigned herself to that end. Need was one thing, but actually acting upon that need was another.

That admission nonetheless didn't keep Meg from wishing she had the nerve to be more like Desiree Moon in her daily life. Meg longed to give Desiree Moon this week, to let her out, so to speak. Let her wear the sexy, silky, off-the-shoulder red dress she'd impulsively bought, then packed. She wanted to be that person, if only for a week.

And why not? Meg wondered consideringly, struck with sudden inspiration. Why couldn't she simply let herself be Desiree Moon this week? No one knew her here at the hotel, there was no one she would be held accountable to. The possibility made her quiver with anticipation. Still…there were other issues.

Meg wasn't ashamed of her work for *Foreplay,* but neither did she wish to become a social pariah and an embarrassment to her family. Regrettably, a seedy connotation went along with what she did. While anything pertaining to sex sold—just look at books, magazines and movies, and the hotter the better—there were still people who considered the topic taboo.

If that wasn't enough motivation, her mother would have a stroke.

But her mother wasn't here, and this was the perfect opportunity, a little-heeded voice persisted. She could do it. There was nothing here to stop her, nothing to prevent her from giving Desiree this week and giving Meg a little excitement in the process. Throw caution to the wind, so to speak. Meg stopped outside her room and fumbled around in her purse for the key card.

"Looks like we're neighbors."

Meg looked up. *Him.* Lust kindled, then detonated, burning her up from the inside out.

It was a sign, Meg decided.

"So we are," she said, the first truly articulate thing she'd managed so far.

Perhaps trust and discretion had nothing to do with her reluctance to engage in a no-strings affair, Meg thought as she watched her mystery man let himself into the room next to hers. Perhaps she'd just never been presented with the proper motivation.

And, as every good pastry chef knew, timing was every bit as important as the ingredients. This week, combined with Mr. Next Door, certainly looked like a recipe for romance to Meg. She'd just bet he'd be delicious.

# 2

*WHAT was she doing in there?*

And what the hell was that noise? To Nick's supreme consternation, Desiree had been in her room for hours. He had heard the unmistakable sound of packages being delivered and enthusiastically opened. She'd oohed and ahhed excitedly at one point, so he assumed she'd gotten something that really pleased her. In addition, room service had been by and her phone had rung at least half a dozen times.

But of all the various noises filtering through the wall, the most intriguing—the most infuriating—had to be the ominous low buzzing hum which now emanated softly from her room.

Nick grimly suspected it was a vibrator.

Exhaling mightily, he shoved away from the connecting door and paced the small area between the foot of his bed and the wall. He speared his fingers through his hair. Irritation and, yes, dammit, lust hurtled through him at the thought of her lying over there doing…things to herself.

Despite the fact that he'd only gotten a vague impression of what she might look like underneath that garb, his imagination nonetheless filled in all the other necessary images, tantalizing him—torturing him—with visions so graphic, so depraved it was all Nick could do to keep from bursting through the door and showing her what the real article could do.

At present, *his* article was about to explode, and all because he suspected her of using a vibrator. One of the toys he detested.

It galled him to no end.

With little effort, Nick could imagine himself being slowly driven insane by presumed acts of carnality. Visions of her naked, lithe, dewy body writhing in ecstasy on that king-sized bed sent his personal mercury into the triple digits. Nick gritted his teeth. And the hell of it was, he didn't even know if she possessed a lithe, dewy body. The unknown combined with his suddenly fertile imagination had turned his brain to mush. He couldn't stand another minute of this, much less a week.

But he had to. The alternative wasn't acceptable.

The infernal buzzing hum suddenly stopped and Nick found himself straining toward the door to listen harder. Several seconds passed, then the sound of running water filled the empty silence. Nick smiled wryly. Atta girl, he thought. Keep the toys clean. At least she practiced good hygiene.

Nick growled under his breath and opted for a shower. A cold one. He needed perspective and listening to every move Desiree made next door and attaching some sort of sexual connotation didn't facilitate clear thinking.

Nick disrobed, then stalked, naked, to the shower. He adjusted the spray, then stepped in. The frigid water stole the breath from his lungs, resulting in a litany of anatomically impossible expletives. He muttered one final oath, then determinedly steered this thinking back to the task at hand.

Before he'd gotten sidetracked by eavesdropping all day, he'd had a perfectly acceptable plan. Nick had decided to put her under surveillance, then stage a few coincidental meetings. To corroborate his in-town-on-business lie, those meetings would have to take place at night. He'd have to quietly hibernate in his room during the day, and plan to see her in the evenings.

According to Ron, the trade show would keep nine-to-five hours, freeing everyone up in the evening to examine the products. Nick chuckled darkly. After five this posh high-rise would turn into Hotel Fornication.

Nevertheless, he sincerely hoped that Desiree would keep to that schedule. It would make his job considerably easier. He assumed that she'd go down to the hotel restaurant in the evenings. Nick would simply turn on the charm, and the rest would be history.

Or so he hoped.

The sooner he got this over with, the better. If things went according to plan, he could be home as early as Wednesday, back to his regular routine, which consisted primarily of work. It had occurred to him that it might not be necessary to stay the entire week. He'd find out if she was a fraud—which he sincerely doubted—then report his findings to Ron. Then he could get back to his productive life at the office. Though he knew Ron needed him, Nick felt off-kilter when he was out of his element. He liked being in the boardroom, closing deals, finalizing mergers, reviewing contracts. Spying on a sex-toy critic, for heaven's sake, was simply not his area of expertise. Still, he'd prepared for this week as best he could.

Nick had read Desiree Moon's critiques and could easily see why she'd become so popular. To begin with, it was obvious that she was educated. She wasn't the stereotypical bored lower-class housewife looking to add a little excitement to her life.

Though Desiree used explicit terms to convey her meaning, she managed to do it in a classy, yet sexy way. She was witty, used a self-deprecating humor that engaged the reader, kept them scrolling the toolbar until she'd said what she wanted to say. Simply put, she not only critiqued, she entertained. In addition to that, her conclusions were thorough and insightful.

Nick couldn't help but wonder if perhaps her assessments of Ron's products weren't right on the money. He certainly hoped not. Nick still had to help him, and by default, protect his mother. His mother had sacrificed enough on her children's behalf—her health—and Nick couldn't let her waste one more penny.

Nick's mother had worked in a sewing factory for

twenty years. She suffered from carpal tunnel syndrome and arthritis, and could barely hold her toothbrush as a result of that labor. His father had been a first-rate mechanic who had worked himself into an early grave.

Like most parents, the Devereaus had wanted a better life for their children, and though they'd had their problems, they'd succeeded, and more. His father had been a wily businessman and had squirreled away enough money to put both Ron and Nick through college, and to see to it that his wife had been provided for.

Nick had used his funds as his father had intended—education. Ron, in another misguided attempt to earn his father's approval, had taken his college fund and opened his own garage. The decision had been a poor one—not Ron's first—and the business went belly-up within a year. Ron had been on a quest to prove himself ever since.

Nick stepped out of the shower, wrapped a towel around his waist and stared into the mirror at his foggy reflection, the familiar guilt settling around him again. He blew out a resigned breath. When this was over, he planned to sit down and have a long talk with his little brother. Ron needed to let go of the past, to forgive their father for his mistakes, and he needed to quit relying on his family for financial support.

To Ron's credit, this particular business had been operating profitably right up until Desiree Moon began to bash his product line on the Internet. Nick had looked at the books, seen a direct correlation.

And, if what Ron suspected were true—if Desiree Moon was a fraud and lacked the experience to critique these products—she needed to be stopped. Right was right and wrong was wrong. If she was making fraudulent claims, then someone needed to put an end to her online career. Nick sighed. Those were a lot of *ifs* and he preferred to deal with certainties. Too bad there weren't any.

Nick heard a door open, then close. Her door.

Shit.

Without the hat and glasses, he didn't know quite what she looked like. Damn. How the hell would he put her under surveillance if he didn't know whom to look for?

Towel still wrapped loosely around his waist, Nick rushed to his own door, pulled it open and stepped out into the hall. He'd taken three steps into the corridor when he realized two things. One, the person in the hall was an old man, and therefore, couldn't be Desiree Moon. Two, he didn't have his key.

A hot oath hissed through his clenched teeth.

To Nick's immense mortification, hotel patrons began to seemingly burst from their rooms like horses from the chutes at the Kentucky Derby. No fewer than five people passed him, giving him curious, look-at-the-pervert stares.

Nick nodded politely to each, heat creeping up his neck. "Stepped into the hall, forgot my key," he muttered inanely.

Given the situation, he had two choices. He could board an elevator and go up to his brother's room, pray that Ron was in and not with the check-in clerk. His stomach knotted in revulsion. Or, he could knock on Desiree's door, then get back into his room via the connecting door.

Ah, hell. He supposed this was one way to speed up the farce. Showing up in nothing but a towel should spark some sort of reaction. Hopefully, the right one.

"I'LL BE CAREFUL. I know all about the undertow. Yes, I brought my sunblock. It's not generic, Mom, it's the good stuff." She could hear the familiar drone of the football game in the background, indicating her father was home from the office. She smiled, thankful that some things in life never changed. "I don't know the number offhand, but I have my cell. Call me on that if anything comes up."

Meg inwardly groaned, regretting the whopping lie she'd fabricated to account for her week-long absence. Her mother, The Chronic Worrier, would fret until Meg arrived safely home from her trip to the "beach."

Still, she could hardly tell her the truth.

*Hey, Ma. Headed into town for a sex-toy trade show. By the way, have I mentioned that I'm a sex-toy critic now? Multi-talented, your daughter is.* Meg chuckled, and then shuddered. Her mother would call an emergency meeting of her prayer group quicker than she could say "Amen." It wouldn't be pretty.

"I don't plan on going to any bars to pick up men, Mom. Yes, I've heard all about the date-rape drug. Listen, Mom—" Meg paused as a knock sounded at her door. Probably another vendor, she surmised. Half listening to more of her mother's concerns, Meg crossed the room, flipped the lock and opened the door. "I'll avoid...strange men, Mom. Bye..." Meg trailed off weakly as her eyes landed on the wet, glistening wall of a spectacularly muscled chest.

She instinctively *knew* whom the chest belonged to, so she didn't waste any time by allowing her gaze to be drawn upward to confirm an identity.

Instead, she took the lucky opportunity to slowly scan and commit to memory each and every golden inch of his impressive torso and all areas south. The chest gave way to a rock-hard, splendidly sculpted abdomen. The desire to learn those ridges, to play them like a harp and listen to the music of his groans of pleasure, the hissing of his breath, was so strong Meg's throat went dry. She wanted to wet her finger, slowly drag it down his belly and swirl it around his navel.

The towel barely clung to lean, narrowed hips, and dipped lower in the front, revealing a gilded treasure trail Meg itched to explore. An impressive bulge created an intriguing terrain across the front of his towel, leaving little doubt that what lay underneath was just as well proportioned as the rest of him. A slow simmer commenced between her thighs and Meg absently licked her lips.

He cleared his throat, forcing her preoccupied gaze

to the northern territory of his face. A slight flush reddened his cheeks and a sheepish grin tugged the corners of his beautiful lips. "I'm locked out of my room," he told her. "Do you mind if I get back in through the connecting door?"

Still bedazzled, Meg blinked. "Connecting door?"

"Our rooms have connecting doors. Haven't you noticed?"

No. She hadn't. Meg glanced behind her to confirm what he said and, sure enough, they did indeed share a connecting door. She didn't know quite what to make of that, and decided to sort the conundrum out when a half-naked man wasn't standing less than two feet from her.

"Would you mind if I came in out of the hall?" he asked, gesturing behind him as a couple of teenagers tittered past. "I'm attracting quite a bit of attention. The kind that could get me arrested."

Meg started. "Oh. Sure. Sorry."

He murmured a thanks as Meg stepped back and allowed him to come in. A clean, masculine fragrance bathed her as he passed, making her knees go weak. Gathering her scattered wits, she hurried to the bed and drew the coverlet over the newest batch of products awaiting her critique, then she doubled back and unlocked her side of the connecting door. She could feel his observant gaze following her.

"Is your side locked?" she asked.

He shoved an impatient hand through his damp hair and swore hotly.

Meg took that as a yes. "Er, why don't you call

down to the front desk and ask someone to come up and open your door? You can wait in here until they arrive.''

"Thanks." He rubbed the back of his neck, then lifted the receiver and dialed the front desk. "I'm really sorry about this. I hope I'm not keeping you from anything."

Meg pretended to check her watch. "I've got a few minutes."

What she really had was a bad case of lust. The man had the best ass she'd ever seen. The damp terrycloth clung to the hard muscles of his butt like butter over warm bread. The finely sculpted muscles of his back glistened with wet droplets and, strangely, Meg found herself consumed with a peculiar urge to nibble a path from his sinewy shoulder up the curiously vulnerable side of his neck.

Heat swamped her, made her breasts heavy, her sex moist. She'd never been more attracted to a man in her life.

"They said they'd send someone up in a moment," he told her. He tightened his towel, glancing about the room as though unsure of what to do or say next.

Making an attempt to be some sort of hostess, Meg hastily scooped up her discarded clothes from the back of the only desk chair. While she'd unpacked all of her things and arranged them to her satisfaction, she'd yet to clear away her dirty clothes. "Have a seat," she offered, summoning a weak smile.

"Thanks." Firmly holding the towel in place, he folded his big frame into the chair.

"So how did you come to get locked out of your room? Like that?" she asked meaningfully, gesturing toward the towel. Her gaze lingered just a fraction longer than necessary.

"I thought I heard someone knock on my door, stepped out into the hall, and the door closed before I could get back in." He lifted one shoulder in a negligent shrug and grinned. "Bet it happens to everyone."

Meg's lips quirked. "I'm sure it does."

"Has it ever happened to you?"

"Nope."

He chuckled, the sound a rich, deep rumble. "You could have lied. I was almost feeling better."

"Sorry." Meg laughed. "Sucks to be you."

His eyes widened at that comment and an outright laugh burst from his chest, making the muscles dance across his abdomen. "Yes, right now, it does sorta suck to be me," he admitted. He extended his hand. "I'm Nick Devereau, by the way."

"Desiree Moon." Meg didn't even hesitate. The lie rolled off her tongue before she'd even realized she'd said it. She didn't know what exactly had possessed her to do that, but it felt incredibly liberating. Wicked. That settled it, Meg decided. For this week only, she would be Desiree Moon and all that persona entailed. A delightful quiver eddied through her.

She took his hand, felt the warm masculine palm

dwarf her smaller one. A zing sparkled up her spine at the contact. Swift. Tingling. Hot.

An intriguing grin claimed his lips and an equally intriguing glint stewed in his sexy, heavy-lidded caramel gaze. "It's a pleasure," he murmured.

Oy. Indeed it was.

A brisk knock sounded at the door, breaking the charged silence.

Meg withdrew her sensitized hand and straightened, reluctant to see him go now that she'd decided to pursue the life of her alter ego. "That'll be for you."

He stood as well and followed her across the room. All the while she was aware of his scrutiny. She could feel that hot stare. It made her all shivery inside.

Meg opened the door so that he could meet the bellhop in the hallway. He paused, then leaned toward her, bringing his tantalizing scent with him. "Thanks, again."

Meg resisted the urge to chew her nail. To bite her fist. "You're welcome."

He turned to go, but seemingly thought better of it and swung back to face her. "Look, could we get a drink later?"

Delight bloomed in her chest, resulting in a small smile. "Sure. Just knock." She gestured toward the connecting door.

He grinned. "Until then."

Meg leaned against the open doorway as he left,

once again mesmerized by his sheer physical beauty. That back. Mercy. Hmm-hmm-hmm. That ass.

Meg straightened, horror dawning.

That ass...had her bra dangling from it.

The hooks had gotten caught in the cloth.

Meg darted out into the hall just as the bellhop planted the key card into the lock. Nick started at her abrupt appearance, then smiled. "Desiree?"

"Nick, uhhh..."

He frowned. "Is something wrong?"

Meg tentatively moved toward him, her gaze darting to where her bra swung drunkenly from the towel. "I, uh...just wanted to let you know I'll be back in my room by eight."

He smiled. "Okay."

The bellhop opened the door and Nick moved to go in. Meg lunged and attempted to covertly snatch her bra. The hook hung stubbornly, and to Meg's slack-jawed astonishment, she not only managed to snag her bra—she snagged his towel as well.

Mortification momentarily burned her cheeks, robbed her of speech. Her gaze was riveted to the only part of his anatomy she'd been unable to properly peruse. Unable to control herself, her lips curled into an appreciative smile.

She'd been right.

He was definitely well proportioned.

# 3

"Flashing her, that's a direct approach. Little forward if you aren't going to seduce her." Ron licked his forefinger, leaned forward and smoothed his eyebrows, then stood back and admired his Fonzie-like reflection. "Myself personally, I like to woo a woman."

"Woo?"

"Yes, woo. It's all part of the chase, the thrill of the hunt."

"This is a woman, Ron. Not an elk, for chrissakes." Dropping into the desk chair in his brother's room, Nick exhaled wearily and rubbed the bridge of his nose. He shuddered to think of what Ron considered wooing. A trip through a drive-thru, then back to his place to show off his lava lamp collection?

"So what's she look like? She a hottie?"

A cloud of dark-chocolate hair, kiss-me mossy-green eyes, smooth skin and a mouth designed for sin flashed through Nick's mind. The hair, the eyes and the skin were pleasing to look at, not remarkable on their own. But the mouth that tied it all together... Damn.

"She's attractive," Nick managed, feeling a tell-tale tightening in his groin.

Ron nodded, apparently satisfied with Nick's assessment. "So, did you sense any interest? She hot for you yet?"

"She's interested," Nick said casually.

And though he had no intention of taking advantage of the situation, she was most definitely hot for him.

Out of all the uncertainties surrounding this scheme, Nick didn't have a doubt about that one fact. She'd practically devoured him with her eyes. That bold green gaze had inventoried every inch of his exposed flesh…and then some.

Nick took care of his body, worked out regularly. He wasn't ignorant of his build and the resulting effect it had on women. He'd been covertly studied before. But he'd never been so intensely scrutinized. Never felt a woman's gaze like that.

Furthermore, when his towel had come off, she'd made no pretense of turning away. Her gaze had dropped to his male equipment, lingered, then she'd had the audacity to smile.

Appreciatively.

Nick found himself equally intrigued and baffled. Baffled because, while he'd gone into her room to set things into motion, he'd been the one knocked for a loop. He'd demonstrated an appalling lack of control, something he never permitted himself to do. Something that mustn't happen again.

Ron grunted as he shoved a foot into his boot, pulling Nick from his reverie. "Listen, if you find anything out tonight that might be helpful, give me a call no matter what time. Keep me posted. I—I need to know what's happening, okay? This is my future we're trying to protect.''

''Sure,'' Nick said, frowning at the desperation in Ron's tone. Ron was very adept at playing him, Nick knew, but he seemed genuinely worried this time. Who knew with Ron? It could only be wishful thinking. ''But I seriously doubt anything will happen tonight. We're just meeting for drinks.''

Ron's brow furrowed. ''Whatever. Just call me. I'm meeting Cindy, but should be back by ten.''

''Cindy?''

Ron smiled. ''The check-in clerk. I'm giving her some free samples.''

Nick's brows rose. On that note, he decided to take his leave. He stood. Desiree had said she'd be back by eight, and it was pushing that now. ''I'm gone,'' Nick told him, heading for the door.

''Work your magic, big brother.'' He paused, giving Nick a small glimpse of Ron's more vulnerable side. ''I've got a lot riding on this.''

That last statement lacked Ron's trademark bravado and, for the first time, Nick detected a hint of fear in his brother's voice. Ron was genuinely afraid of losing this business. Fear was the beginning of wisdom. Given that, perhaps the end would justify the means.

Nick fervently hoped so.

''MR. KENT will be arriving tomorrow. He rarely attends these trade shows, but he's very anxious to meet you.''

"I'm looking forward to meeting him as well," Meg murmured. Marcus Kent, the senior editor for *Foreplay* magazine, had recently decided to personally handle Desiree Moon's reviews. They had communicated via e-mail and telephone, but had never met in person.

"Do you have everything you need?" Ann Dolan, Marcus's assistant asked. "Everything in your room to your liking?" She smiled. "You're our star, you know. I was told to keep you happy."

Meg laughed. "I'm happy and I have everything I need, thank you."

"Good." Ann sighed. "Well, we've covered your schedule, outlined your workshop. I think we've done everything we were supposed to do." She quirked a brow. "Would you like to go to the lounge and get a drink?"

Meg hesitated. She nudged up her sleeve and checked her watch. "Er, actually I'm supposed to meet someone."

Ann's eyes widened. "Oh, of course," she said knowingly. "You brought Antonio. Naturally, you would. Duh." Ann popped her forehead with the palm of her hand. "This is a trade show. You're here to critique. How else would you…well, you know?"

"I, uh—"

She nodded approvingly. "Mr. Kent will like that," Ann confided. "The majority of our critics are women. He's been very interested in getting a fresh hetero male perspective. I'm supposed to call in tonight with a report. I'll be sure and let him know that you brought your partner with you. He's been anxious to meet the legendary Antonio,'' she shared with a droll smile. "We all have."

Meg's insides froze. Antonio? The fictitious Antonio? "Well," Meg faltered, "I'm not sure that my, uh— That Antonio would be comfortable talking about our—"

"Oh, don't worry about that. Mr. Kent will put him right at ease. He has a way of doing that."

That would be fine, Meg thought, if she had an Antonio to put at ease! How on earth would she get out of this mess? She'd have to think of something, and quick. The man would be here tomorrow, expecting to meet her...and dear old Antonio. Dread mushroomed inside her. Her dinner—which she'd enjoyed—curdled in her stomach.

"Well, I won't keep you," Ann told her, standing. She drew her purse from the back of the chair. "I'm sure you're anxious to get upstairs and, er, get started."

Meg managed a weak goodbye. Her mind whirled. Actually, she had been anxious to get back upstairs so that she could wait for Nick. But now... Now, she had a mess to deal with. It had never occurred to her that she would need to bring a partner, that they would expect her to have him here with her.

But it should have.

This was a sex-toy trade show and she, a critic.

Meg absently worried her bottom lip. Well, she

would think of something. She would make up a lie.
She'd simply tell them that poor Antonio had been
called home on an emergency. His mother was ill,
his house had been hit by a tornado, his brother
needed a kidney transplant and he was the only
match. Something. Meg snorted at the extreme scenarios her desperate mind created. In for a penny, in
for a pound, she thought. Might as well make it a
good one.

Meg stood and refused to think about it anymore.
She would handle it in the morning. Right now she
needed to get back upstairs. To wait for Nick. A
tingle of excitement bubbled through her.

Though the meal had been delicious, she'd barely
been able to eat. It had been a long time since she'd
had anything that remotely resembled a date—she'd
been too busy double-timing it up her career path to
enjoy any sort of social life—and something about
this guy... Meg paused consideringly. Physical attraction aside, something about this guy seemed different. She didn't know exactly what yet, but she
intuitively knew that the potential for something extraordinary had been presented to her and she didn't
intend to waste it.

Besides, now that she'd decided to momentarily
ditch her ho-hum life and trade it in for the week for
an exciting one, she couldn't wait to get started. Meg
shuddered to think about what that said about the life
she'd led to date, that she'd be so willing to abandon
it. True, since the scholarship fiasco she'd forsaken

all men and pursued her career with single-minded determination. But had it really been that bad? That boring? That empty?

Yes.

With that disturbing realization in mind, Meg hurried to her room. Rather than sit on the end of the bed and twiddle her thumbs while she waited for him, she took the opportunity to straighten up. Meg couldn't stand clutter, liked her surroundings balanced, harmonized and color-coordinated. In her line of work, presentation was almost as important as the quality of the dish she prepared and that mentality had spilled over into other areas of her life. She'd been told she was maddeningly meticulous. Meg grinned. She just considered herself thorough.

Less than five minutes passed when a soft knock sounded at the connecting door. So he'd been just as anxious. Meg felt a grin tug at her lips. Taking a fortifying breath, she smoothed her jacket and opened the door.

"Hi," she managed. He looked devastating. He wore khaki trousers, a white oxford shirt and a come-hither smile that melted Meg's insides.

"Ready?"

"Sure."

Meg slipped her key card back into her purse and allowed him to escort her from the room. The sheer size of him struck her again. Her head lay a good two inches below his shoulder. Though totally against her feminist nature, the thought made her feel safe. Protected. This was the sort of man that a cave woman would want to take as a husband. A big, tough, muscled warrior who would defend and protect.

A ribbon of heat curled through her. Need consumed her, made her knees momentarily go weak. Hell, they hadn't even made it to the elevator and yet she found herself hit with the insane notion to skip the drinks altogether and drag him back to her room.

Which was ridiculous, of course, because Meg had never dragged any man to her bed, much less a complete stranger. And while this man happened to be the answer to her every carnal fantasy, he was still a stranger.

He was just a stranger she was impossibly attracted to.

But she didn't have to consider what Meg would do, she reminded herself, only what Desiree would do, and this week she was Desiree. A sly smile curled her lips as she cast a sidelong glance at her companion. The possibilities were endless.

Nick guided her into the elevator with a hand at her elbow. The minimal contact nonetheless ignited a sparkler of pleasure low in her belly. "Did you enjoy your dinner?" he asked, pulling Meg from her mental musings.

"I did," she replied. "What about you? Have you eaten?"

"I ordered room service."

Well, that took care of that line of conversation.

Now what were they going to talk about? Meg wondered as the silence yawned between them.

"Fifty percent chance of rain tonight," he remarked casually.

"Is that right?"

He rocked back on his heels. "So I heard."

"I like rain," Meg replied, her lips curling into a small grin.

"I do, too."

"Makes me sleepy."

The elevator glided to a smooth halt. He twined his fingers with hers and waited for the doors to open. "That covers the traditional pleasantries," he murmured, his voice a smooth decadent rumble. "How about we move on to a more interesting topic of conversation."

"Like what?" Meg chuckled.

His lazy, half-lidded gaze captured hers. "You."

Oh, he was smooth. Definitely out of her league and she out of her element. What on earth was she doing? "You'd be sadly disappointed if you thought I'd be a more interesting topic of conversation."

He gave her a sideways glance. "I doubt it."

They strolled into the lounge and found a secluded table tucked past the bar. In a gentlemanly fashion Meg hadn't witnessed in ages, Nick obligingly pulled out her chair.

"What would you like to drink?" he asked.

"Chardonnay."

"It'll be quicker if I go to the bar." He squeezed her shoulder. "Don't go away."

Like hell, Meg thought as she watched him cross the room. Once again she found herself thrown into the grip of another bout of yearning. The man walked with an economy of movement, languid yet purposeful. Nick Devereau was obviously a man who felt comfortable in his own skin.

Meg had always prided herself on her ability to size a person up. She read confidence in the breadth of his shoulders, a smidge of arrogance in the tilt of his jaw and—the most distracting of all—the invitation to sin in those warm, heavy-lidded butterscotch eyes.

While Desiree Moon might long to throw caution to the wind, Meg Sugarbaker was still more than a little gun-shy. She'd been burned before and repercussions for that one stupid mistake had blistered her enough to make her very cautious. The last time she'd dropped her guard she'd lost a scholarship that would have saved her thousands of dollars and garnered respect in the snobbish circles of haute cuisine. She'd also been made a laughingstock. Though she was more mature now and circumstances were different, old habits died hard. Meg chose her company carefully, kept her circle tight.

But hadn't she decided not to worry about Meg's concerns this week? Hadn't she decided to *be* Desiree Moon? If that were the case, then she shouldn't be bound by all the old doubts, reservations and insecurities. She should simply live in the moment and see where this week took her. And she'd only have this week. Once it was over, it would be back to good old Meg. The thought struck a curious pang of regret, but Meg forced it away and concentrated on the present.

After all, this was the first time she'd been out on anything that remotely resembled a date in ages, and Nick Devereau was by far the most handsome man she'd ever laid eyes on. She would simply enjoy herself and the rest would take care of itself.

Resigned to that end, Meg took a moment to survey the bar. Though relatively early, a sizable crowd had gathered. A soulful jazz tune emanated from hidden speakers, creating an intimate bare-your-soul atmosphere. A smoky haze swirled near the ceiling, casting an eerie glow in the dimly lit lounge.

Nick returned with their drinks. "Now where were we? Oh, yes. You were going to tell me about yourself."

Her gaze tangled with his. "I was?"

"Certainly. We decided you were a more interesting topic of conversation than the weather."

Meg grinned wryly. Aside from the fact that she was a sex-toy critic, there was absolutely nothing interesting about her life. She was a single, twenty-seven-year-old pastry chef, a frustrated semivirgin who owned a small patio home in a middle-class subdivision. Rather than succumb to the old-maid cat cliché, she'd bought a gerbil. Whoopee. Didn't she live life in the fast lane?

Well, that would all change when she pulled together the tuition and travel fees for the school in Paris. Her dream was almost in reach. Just a few more months and she'd be a true cosmopolitan woman.

But she wasn't yet.

"No," she clarified, drawing in a cautious breath. "*You* decided I would be a more interesting topic of conversation."

He shrugged noncommittally. "Semantics. Tell me about yourself."

Another interesting discovery, Meg thought, unreasonably impressed. Nick Devereau didn't seem to have any intention of dominating their conversation with the usual bullshit bravado men normally felt compelled to impart. He seemed genuinely interested in her. Meg couldn't help but be impressed. "What do you want to know?" she asked.

"Everything."

Meg chuckled. "Not much, eh?"

"Why don't we do a little Q&A? Tit for tat, so to speak." He stilled, studying her intently. "If I ask something that's too personal or something you don't want to answer, then just say 'pass.' I'll do the same to any question you ask me."

Meg mulled it over. "Okay," she conceded grudgingly. "Sounds fair."

"What do you do for a living?"

Hell. Meg mentally rolled her eyes. He would ask that first. While the sex-toy critic job was more interesting, it wasn't her primary source of income. Besides, she didn't know how to do the Heimlich and he'd probably choke if she imparted that little factoid. "I'm a pastry chef," Meg answered. "What do you do?"

He sipped his whiskey. "I'm an attorney. A pastry chef," he repeated, seemingly intrigued. "That's a great deal more interesting than the weather. What restaurant?"

Hmmm. Too personal, Meg decided. Too risky as well. Though unlikely, she still might discover some hideous character flaw. She might not want him knowing where she worked. "Sorry, I'll pass on that one," she told him. An earlier suspicion surfaced and she regarded him shrewdly. "Are you gay?"

He strangled on his whiskey. "Wh-what? No! Why?" His brows winged up his forehead. "Do I— Do I act gay?"

"That's two questions," Meg pointed out as she resisted the urge to laugh. His abrupt, outraged, vehement "no" certainly left no doubt that he was straight. "I'll answer the last question. No, you don't act gay…but you seem too good to be true." Meg narrowed her gaze, studied him thoughtfully. "Are you married?"

"No." A hint of humor danced in his eyes and a bit of self-satisfaction clung to the edges of his half-hearted smile. "Why do you think I'm too good to be true?"

That had been too telling a remark, Meg thought ruefully. She'd have to watch herself. Pass or be forthright? She chose forthright. It seemed the Desiree thing to do. "Because you're a seemingly sane, heterosexual, unmarried, attractive professional over thirty.'' Meg leaned forward. "Do you live with your mother?''

A burst of laughter erupted from his chest. "No. Are you married?''

Meg shook her head. "Does mental illness run in your family?''

"No.'' His gaze captured hers and he lowered his voice. "Do you realize you are the most entertaining woman I've met in a long time?''

Meg blushed, pleased at the unexpected compliment. "No, I didn't. Are you currently taking any prescription medications, mood elevators, antidepressants?''

The perpetual grin kicked up around the edges. "No. Would you like to dance?''

Meg's drink stalled halfway to her mouth. "Er...'' Meg glanced around the increasingly crowded room. Some industrious patrons had shoved several tables out of the way and had created a makeshift dance floor.

"Didn't catch a 'pass' or a 'no', so I'll take that as a yes.'' Nick stood and drew her to her feet, then gently tugged her toward the dance floor. Within seconds, she found herself curled into his masculine embrace. His warm palms lay anchored at her hips and it seemed the most natural thing in the world to twine her arms around his neck. Her head fit perfectly in the hollow under his chin. His scent, a clean woodsy fragrance, swirled around her senses, enveloping her in a sensual haze. The music throbbed around them and for Meg, the rest of the room simply faded away.

For all intents and purposes, they were glued from the knee up, and the contact had all but set Meg aflame. Her blood pulsed warmly in her veins, pooled at her womanly center. The desire for release, the unequivocal need, spiraled inside her, an ever-tightening coil.

She felt his breath stir near her ear. "You're a good dancer. And you smell wonderful."

"Thank you," she murmured, impossibly warming more with the compliment. "You dance well yourself." She paused. "Did you learn how at your anger management classes?"

His chuckle vibrated through her, and she could feel his smile against her hair. "Still looking for faults, I see. Can't you just accept the fact that I'm perfect?"

Meg giggled. "Aha!"

He drew back to look at her. "Aha, what?"

"You're not perfect." She sniffed. "A perfect man would never be so conceited."

"Touché," he said, laughing.

As much as she dreaded it, Meg knew the time had come to bid him good-night.

While she still would.

While she still *could.*

Her shoulders rounded with a sigh as the song drew to a close. "It's getting late," she confided regretfully. "I've got an early morning."

"I do, too. We should probably head back upstairs."

Meg nodded, pleased to note that he didn't seem

any more eager to end their date than she did. The trip to the room went entirely too fast for Meg's liking, but she knew she shouldn't linger. It had been a pleasant evening and, other than that last dance, she'd managed to keep from launching herself into his arms. Or into his lap. Or at his mouth.

Which would have been entirely too easy.

Meg paused outside her door and turned to face him. Lashes at half-mast, those butterscotch orbs had darkened into a warm caramel. Meg suppressed a shiver. Her mouth dried…watered. Her gaze strayed to his full, firm lips and, with effort, she swallowed. "I've had a really good time tonight. Thank you."

"You're welcome." His gaze dropped to her mouth. Lingered. He cleared his throat. "Are you leaving tomorrow?"

Meg shook her head. "I'll be here all week."

He released a small breath. "Me, too. Can I see you again?"

A bud of pleasure unfurled in her chest. "Sure."

The space between them had mysteriously lessened, Meg noted as her gaze once again returned to his lips.

"Same time tomorrow night?"

"It's a date."

"Then let's seal it with a kiss." He framed her face gently and his mouth descended to hers. His lips were firm, yet soft, and deliciously warm, and the taste of whiskey still clung to them. Meg moaned with pleasure, sank more firmly against him and angled her head to grant him better access.

*Mamma-mia.* This man knew how to kiss.

He knew precisely how to alternate pressure, how to suckle, how to explore the ultra-sensitive recesses of her mouth. His tongue curled around hers, plundered in and out, back and forth, and while his mouth laid siege to hers, his hands had started an equally thorough expedition.

But that was okay, because hers had too.

Meg mapped his chest with her palms, felt the hard muscles bunch beneath her hands, vibrate at her touch. When she'd gotten her feel for those areas, she moved north, to his massive shoulders, then on to his nape, where she curled her fingers into the silky tawny locks.

Nick's hands were equally eager. He palmed her ribs, barely thumbing the undersides of her breasts. *Up! Up!* Meg wanted to scream. Her nipples ached with need, puckered for attention. She longed to feel his mouth anchored there, feeding on her as his lips fed now on her mouth.

His big warm hands traveled round the small of her back and settled on her rump. He squeezed her there, drew her upward and aligned her so that she came navel to zipper with the evidence of his arousal. Desire flooded her sex, moisture drenched her feminine folds. Nick swallowed her groan of want as she moved impatiently against him. Need clawed at her, consumed her, made her wiggle shamelessly against him. She wanted—

"Didn't we get you a room?"

The vaguely familiar humorous male voice shattered the sensual fog and Meg and Nick broke apart guiltily. Meg turned…and came face-to-face with Ann and a man whom she could only assume was Marcus Kent.

Mortification glued her tongue to the roof of her mouth. "I—uh."

The man extended his hand. "Marcus Kent. You're Desiree, right?"

Meg nodded, still bewildered. "Right."

"I've been looking forward to meeting you." His gaze bounced to Nick, glinted with something strangely akin to hunger. "And your significant other, Antonio."

Nick frowned. "An—"

"It's so nice to finally meet you, Mr. Kent," Meg rushed to impart before Nick could finish.

Mr. Kent reluctantly returned his attention to Meg. "I know that you have a busy day tomorrow, Desiree. But at some point over the next week, I'd really like to meet with you and your partner. I've been anxious to get a hetero male opinion of some of those new products we're reviewing." He eagerly turned to Nick. "For instance, those new penis jelly rings. Man to man, Antonio," he confided, edging closer to Nick, "do they really prolong an erection?"

Nick's eyes bulged. "Wh—"

"We'll have to get back to you on that, Mr. Kent. It was a pleasure meeting you." Meg crammed the key card in the lock, shoved the door open and herded Nick inside. "See you tomorrow," Meg trilled amiably. She sagged against the door, then turned to face Nick.

Meg winced at his thunderstruck expression. "Sorry about that."

"Penis jelly ring? What the hell is that man talking about?"

"Dunno," Meg lied, studiously avoiding his gaze. She opened her side of the connecting door and nimbly guided Nick to it.

Gone was the jovial charmer. The shrewd attorney had taken his place. "I suspect you do. And why did he call me 'your partner'?"

Inwardly, Meg sighed. There was no way around it. She had to level with him. Especially if she thought he might be persuaded to don the role of her partner while they were here. She'd considered it. What choice did she have now that they'd been seen together? The he's-gone-to-donate-a-kidney story certainly wouldn't fly now—they'd see him around the hotel.

Honestly, who would have thought that one cocktailed trip through cyberspace in search of a vibrator to remedy her perpetually aroused state would result in this chaos?

Meg nervously cleared her throat. "Okay, here's the truth. *I am* a pastry chef." The rest she spewed out in a rush. "I'm-also-an-online-sex toy-critic-in-town-for-a-trade-show-and-that-man-in-the-hall-was-my-editor-and-he-thinks-that-you're-my-partner-Antonio-whom-I've-been-sleeping-with-while-

I've-been-critiquing-various-products-over-the-past-several-months. Understand?''

If possible, his dumbfounded expression intensified. ''No, I—'' Meg leaned forward and captured his lips with hers. She threw every bit of her yearning into the kiss—every ounce of want—then abruptly drew back, making him stagger forward. ''G'night,'' she murmured breathlessly. ''We'll discuss this later.''

Then she closed the door on his gorgeous, thoroughly bewildered face.

# 4

ASTOUNDED, NICK BLINKED as the door closed in his face. Blinked again. It took a moment to realize that Desiree wasn't going to open the door and offer any other explanation for the bizarre episode in the hall. Numb with shock, Nick entered his own room, crossed to the bed and collapsed onto the mattress. His breath left him in a whoosh.

What in God's name had just happened? Since he'd agreed to this maniacal plan of Ron's, Nick's predictable, uncluttered life—which he, for the most part, enjoyed—had made a left turn at Strange and exited onto Bizarre.

If he'd heard and interpreted Desiree's hurried soliloquy correctly, that man in the hall was laboring under the incorrect assumption that his name was Antonio, he and Desiree were lovers—had been lovers for several months—and that, *he,* Nick Devereau, enjoyed kinky sex and had used something called a penis jelly ring to prolong his erection.

A band of tension tightened around Nick's skull. The hard-on he'd enjoyed as a result of that mind-blowing kiss promptly wilted.

How had this happened? Nick wondered. How had

his plan gone so totally awry? Admittedly, it had never been the best plan. Nick knew that. But, in the end, what choice had he had? Guilt had gotten the better of Nick and had propelled him into action once again on his brother's behalf.

He'd had to help Ron.

And while his "charm her" strategy wasn't exactly the noblest cause of action, the woman in question was an adult. She could refuse to be charmed, he'd reasoned when his conscience had howled its disapproval. She didn't have to even give him the time of day.

But all of that had been when the woman had simply been a target—not a person.

Not *her*.

Unbidden, an image of Desiree rose in his mind. That smooth heart-shaped face surrounded by all that silky, dark-brown hair. Those compelling, mossy-green eyes which alternately glittered with humor and darkened with desire. They were a kaleidoscope of emotion, a mantrap.

But her mouth…

Nick closed his eyes. Astonishingly, the pleasure of kissing her had to be one of the single most erotic things he'd ever experienced. That plump, plum-soft bottom lip, the rasp of her tongue against his as he plundered the silky recesses of her mouth. Nick swallowed.

He'd been so caught up in the kiss—so caught up in feeling those full, ripe lips tasting his—that he'd come within a gnat's ass of backing her against the wall and taking her right there.

In the damned hall.

Which was ridiculous because he firmly intended not to stage an all-out seduction. He would not take her to bed. He'd only come here to get close to her, to see if she was indeed the fraud Ron thought her to be. Sleeping with her—no matter how badly he might want to—was simply out of the question. Nick had compromised his honor enough. He would not destroy it completely by seducing a woman on purpose under false pretenses.

Still, he'd never been so turned on, so desperate to plant himself between a woman's thighs.

Undoubtedly, if Marcus Kent hadn't come along, that's exactly where he'd be right now. Between her thighs, pumping in and out, deep and hard until they both were wrung dry and sated with relief.

Naked limbs and tangled sheets, the musky tang of sex in the air.

Then, she'd kiss him again with those unbelievably carnal lips, he'd harden—without the aid of a penis jelly ring, he thought darkly—and they'd start all over again.

No! No, they wouldn't, dammit! He wouldn't allow it.

Visions of those previous thoughts rebelliously arose in Nick's tortured mind and he winced as he once again stiffened to the point of pain. Disgusted, he laced his fingers behind his head and stared at the ceiling, mentally willing the futile erection away.

Short of taking matters into his own hands, so to speak, there was nothing left to do.

Nick gritted his teeth and flatly refused to even entertain the thought. He hadn't had to resort to masturbation for relief since he'd ditched the orthodontic headgear and gotten his first car.

He certainly didn't have any intention of doing it now.

He could handle the frustration. Really. Any minute now, this raging erection would wither and he could quit thinking about what it would be like to sheath himself in Desiree's heat. To feel those small capable hands of hers gliding over his skin. Clutching his ass, urging him on as he pistoned in and out of her hot, velvety channel.

To Nick's supreme irritation, a low-buzzing hum suddenly broke the tense silence. A grim, humorless smile turned his lips and a bark of laughter erupted from his throat.

Another fantasy took hold. He closed his eyes and groaned. Swore. Groaned again.

Imagined her flushed skin. All that glorious hair fanned out on a stark white pillow. Long, bare limbs writhing on top of crisp sheets. Her small even teeth sunk into that amazingly full bottom lip. Naked, puckered breasts. A tangle of moistened chocolate curls at the junction of her creamy thighs…

*Buzzzzzzzzzzzz.*

…her clever fingers massaging the secret bud nestled like a treasure in her wet, feminine folds. Arched neck, a moan of pleasure…

A bead of sweat broke out on Nick's brow. Frustration welled, peaked. He resisted the urge to gnash his teeth. To scream.

*Buzzzzzzzzzz.*

Ah, hell. With a defeated sigh, he lowered his zipper and took matters into his own hands.

SHE'D PROBABLY NEVER SEE HIM again, Meg reflected gloomily as she applied her mascara. She blinked, satisfied that she'd coated each lash and slipped the slim tube back into its place in her makeup case. Going to the trouble of getting ready for their date seemed like a monumental waste of time considering he'd most likely departed the hotel first thing this morning, or at the very least had moved to a different room.

But Meg went through the motions anyway on the off chance that he still planned to keep their date. After all, he hadn't called to cancel. He struck her as the type who'd extend such a courtesy.

When she'd returned to her room this afternoon after attending her trade-show duties, she'd fully expected to hear his regrets on her voice mail. But she hadn't. Nor had she heard any activity in his room. No TV. Not so much as the flush of a commode. It had been eerily quiet.

Honestly, though, if he stood her up, could she really blame him? A sigh seeped past her lips. Despite the fact that they'd had a great time and had obviously clicked on several different levels, he'd been asked a very personal question—about his erection, for pity's sake!—by a complete stranger.

And it was all her fault.

Of all the rotten luck, Meg silently railed. If it had been anyone but Marcus Kent who'd caught the two of them in the hall, she wouldn't be in this predicament.

And it was a predicament. As screwed-up as a soup sandwich.

Marcus had cornered her downstairs again this afternoon, extolling his unending delight over meeting Antonio and getting his perspective on all the products she'd been critiquing. The curiously effeminate man had practically rubbed his greedy little hands in anticipation. He simply couldn't wait. And, wouldn't it be wonderful if Antonio could start critiquing, too? Do a *He Said, She Said*-type review and run them together? Run their pictures beside their column, just like Ann Landers?

Oh, I don't know, Meg thought sarcastically. Lemme think about that a minute. No!

Meg pulled in a shaky breath. No, it would not be wonderful. Their pictures? Please. When hell froze over. She didn't even use her own name, for heaven's sake. Why the hell would she want her picture up there for the entire world to see? *Hey, Ma. Check out this url. www.yourdaughterthenympho.com.*

A hysterical bubble of laughter fizzled up her throat. This was turning into her worst nightmare. If it weren't for Paris—for the opportunity to study

with Pierre—despite the fact that she enjoyed critiquing, Meg would give notice and head straight
back to her unsuspecting virtually stress-free life.
There was a lot to be said for peace of mind, Meg
decided, and ever since Marcus had seen Meg in the
hall with Nick, her peace of mind had been shattered.

Marcus had lots of ideas, all of which had begun
to make Meg physically ill from thinking about them.
Because each one was worse than the last—and they
all involved the partner she didn't have, but seemed
she would be forced, in short order, to get.

Meg had gone over it and over it in her head and,
if Nick showed up tonight, she'd have no choice but
to ask him to pose as her lover. A shiver of need
accompanied that thought. But Marcus had seen him,
would inevitably see him around the hotel. It was
either ask Nick to masquerade as Antonio, or confess
to Marcus that she didn't have a partner at all.

Regrettably, neither scenario was very attractive,
and if she didn't ask Nick, she could kiss going to
Paris next summer goodbye.

She'd have to ask Nick.

He'd probably say no, but what the hell? At this
point, other than her job, her dream and a-potential-
boyfriend/chance-of-a-lifetime/weeklong-tryst-with-
the-sexiest-man-she'd-ever-laid-eyes-on what did she
have to lose?

Admittedly, Meg had been unreasonably attracted
to Nick from the start. She'd practically gone into a
molecular meltdown from the moment he'd first
stepped into the elevator with her. Something about

him tripped every single one of her triggers. She didn't know what exactly and she certainly didn't know why.

But she'd never craved a man so much, never turned into a single throbbing nerve of need by simply staring at a man's lips before. All of these little indicators should have tipped her off, should have prepared her for The Kiss.

But they hadn't.

Meg had been within a millimeter of orgasm when Marcus Kent had interrupted them. One more wiggle—mercy—one more slip of his tongue into her mouth and she would have climaxed.

Right there in the hall.

Still fully clothed.

Thanks to a man, not a toy.

Dammit, she wanted that orgasm! It was hers. She'd waited her entire adult life for a real, male-induced orgasm and Marcus Kent had robbed her of it. Meg felt like stamping her foot, like a kid whose favorite toy had been stolen by a schoolyard bully. She wanted to scream in frustration. She settled for a whimper of regret.

Now, who knew what would happen? Even if Nick did keep their date, she seriously doubted he'd agree to be her pseudo lover. And even if he did, look at the torture she would be in for. They'd be forced to talk about the product line, the toys...sex...all the time. She'd have to prep him, give him a crash course in Sex 101. The thought made Meg smile.

She—a virgin in every sense but the word—giving him sex lessons.

Like he'd need any. Meg snorted. She knew without a doubt Nick Devereau had plenty of experience when it came to bed play. If his kiss had been any indication of the rest of his abilities, then he undoubtedly had been pleasuring women since puberty. Highly motivated libido or no, Meg knew it took an extreme amount of talent to make a woman almost come with nothing but a kiss.

Meg shrugged into her dress, then fastened a pair of strappy sandals onto her feet. If he didn't stand her up, maybe she'd get lucky and he'd kiss her again.

"So, LET ME MAKE SURE that I've got this straight. You want me to pretend that we're lovers, to pretend that you and I have used—do use, on a regular basis—sex toys when we make love? That I'm this Antonio person?"

Desiree swallowed. Nodded jerkily. Amazingly, she seemed genuinely embarrassed. "That about sums it up, yes."

"You are a sex-toy critic for an online magazine and you're here for the trade show that's going on in the hotel?"

This time she cleared her throat. "Right. I had to come alone, and then my boss saw me necking in the hall with you... He assumed you were Antonio." She shrugged. "I'm kinda in a bind."

The irony wasn't lost on Nick. Ron had asked him

to be her lover in fact—which he'd refused to do—and now she'd asked him to be her lover in theory.

The situation had just taken another absurd turn, but one that would benefit Ron's cause. It would certainly be easier to gather the ammunition to discredit her if they were working so closely together. Playing the part of her sex-toy critique partner would undoubtedly result in togetherness, probably more than he could comfortably handle, Nick realized as a finger of trepidation slid down his spine.

And while he'd imagined many scenarios for how this date would proceed, Desiree Moon asking him to pose as her sex-toy critique partner had never been one of them.

Nick lounged back in his chair, considering her thoughtfully. That explained why she'd seemed so relieved when he'd shown up at her door. She hadn't been anxious to see him—she needed something from him.

To Nick's surprise, he found himself unreasonably perturbed. The idea that she'd resort to using him to keep her critiquing job shouldn't bother him, considering he was the one with the ulterior motive. He'd only come to the hotel with the purpose of gathering evidence for Ron, to ruin her credibility in that very field.

But it did.

Some sort of revelation he didn't wish to pursue lurked in that thought, so Nick—being Nick—bullied it aside and focused on the positive.

This could definitely work to his advantage. True,

pretending firsthand experience with questionable things such as penis jelly rings would be intensely humiliating and against every natural instinct he had as a man.

But it would even the playing field.

He could help Desiree while gleaning his information for Ron. Then he wouldn't be the only one benefiting from this insane, totally ridiculous scheme. She would, too.

He mentally shrugged. He could work with that. In fact, now that he'd boxed his misgivings into a neat little package which no longer concerned him, Nick felt more comfortable going into stealth mode. Just to punish her for making him feel so out of sorts, he pulled an Emeril and kicked it up a notch.

"Okay," he said at last.

Those impossibly green eyes rounded in relief. "You'll do it?"

"Why wouldn't I?" Nick lowered his voice to an intimate level, and blatantly perused every inch of her. Her mouth, the subtle curve of her jaw, the slender column of her throat. How would she taste there? he wondered. "You're a gorgeous, intelligent female whom I'm intensely attracted to," he murmured. "You just offered me the opportunity to discuss sex with you at length." He lifted a shoulder in a negligent shrug. "Why wouldn't I agree?"

She gulped. "You realize that Marcus will put you on the spot? Expect you to answer very personal, potentially embarrassing questions?"

Nick nodded. "It's worth the trade-off."

"Penis jelly rings are just the tip of the iceberg," she warned.

"I can handle it." He hoped. Damn. What could possibly be worse than penis jelly rings? Did he really want to know? No matter. Undoubtedly, he'd find out.

Seemingly satisfied, Desiree leaned back into the barrel-backed chair in the lounge and absently ringed the rim of her glass with her index finger. She wore a tangerine-colored tank dress that swung loosely around her thighs and the sexiest little sandals he'd ever seen. Nick imagined he could have her out of the dress in less than three seconds. She could leave the shoes on.

Bloody hell. He had to stop thinking like this. He had to—

"Antonio?" Desiree sing-songed as she wiggled her fingers at him. "Yoo-hoo?"

Nick blinked. "Come again?"

Smiling, Desiree tsked. "You have to remember that you're Antonio now. It'll look funny if Marcus or Ann address you and you act like you don't know who they're talking to."

"Right," Nick said, feeling foolish. "Forgive me. I'm not used to answering to anything but my own name. Funny how that works."

Desiree chuckled. "Trust me, when this is over, you'll be glad that you haven't used your real name."

Nick stilled. For the first time since he'd met her, it occurred to him that he didn't know her real name.

"You use a pseudonym?" he asked lightly, though he knew the answer to that question. He simply wanted to see if she'd tell him the truth. To see if she trusted him enough to give him her real name.

Which was ridiculous, Nick chided himself. She shouldn't trust him, was right to guard her privacy. Why did he keep testing her character when he was the one here with the hidden agenda? Sheesh. He had to get a grip.

"I do," she replied hesitantly.

When it became obvious she didn't intend to share her real identity, Nick posed another question. "When this week is over will you give me your real name?"

Her slim shoulders lifted in a shrug and she regarded him with a sexy enigmatic gaze. "Depends."

"On what?"

"On whether you'll still want it at the end of the week."

"I will," he promised. And truer words have never been spoken, Nick realized. A curious tightening squeezed his chest, not altogether pleasant.

The silence lengthened and it occurred to Nick that the conversation had become too serious. "So." He blew out a breath, summoned an amiable smile. "How did you come up with the name 'Desiree Moon'?"

"Can't remember," she said matter-of-factly. "I was drunk."

Nick chuckled again. God, this woman was full of surprises. "Drunk?"

"Yep. Totally cocktailed. I applied for the critic position online, made up the name, everything." Sighing, she rested her cheek against her palm. "While I was drunk. Things just sort of escalated from there."

You could drive a truck through the hole in that explanation, but if she didn't feel inclined to fill it in, then he certainly didn't intend to ask. Pastry chef to sex-toy critic was quite a leap. Nick had wondered how she'd gotten started doing something that, at times, seemed so totally out of character. She baffled him. Intrigued him. Made him laugh.

"So—" she sighed "—are you absolutely sure that you want to go through with this?"

Nick nodded. "Sure."

"Then we'd better get started prepping you. I don't know exactly when Marcus is going to want to see us, but if I had to guess, I'd say it'll probably be sometime Thursday."

Nick's brow wrinkled with confusion. It was only Monday night. "We need to start prepping me now?" he asked. "How much am I going to have to learn?"

"A lot," she said meaningfully, as if Nick didn't have the first clue about sex. "He's going to expect you to know about virtually every product that I've critiqued. Let's see," she mused, tapping her finger against her chin. "I have my journal, so we can go back over everything that I've done up to this point. Then we can go through all of the products that I've got up in my room. That should be enough to make sure you pass muster.''

Nick blinked. She made it sound like a damned arsenal. Another question surfaced. ''You keep a journal?''

''Yes.''

''What for?'' he asked uneasily.

''I like to write down my impressions of a product as soon as I finish using it. That way when I go back to write my critique, I have more to go on.'' She paused. ''It's not just whether an item is stimulating or not. I critique everything about a product. Size, texture, scent…everything.''

He'd known she was thorough. He'd gleaned that much on his own. To Nick's displeasure, a vision of her giving him the old heave-ho immediately after they'd had sex to write in her journal suddenly filled his head. What would she write about him? His size? His texture? His scent? Or, God forbid, his performance?

A fist of anxiety tightened his gut. Nothing, Nick reminded himself, because he wasn't going to sleep with her. He wouldn't allow things to progress that far.

Nick had never doubted himself when it came to pleasuring a woman. He was an excellent lover, had been told so on many occasions. He had absolutely no reason to suspect that, were they to ever make love, he'd be unable to satisfy her.

Furthermore, since he'd met Desiree, his thoughts had been consumed with what it would be like to taste every inch of her, to bury himself so deeply inside her it would take dynamite to blast him out. In his dreams—the only place he could have her— he'd put that curvy little compact body of hers into more positions than a side show contortionist.

But in those dreams, it had never occurred to him that she'd be critiquing him.

Quite frankly, he didn't like the idea at all. He wouldn't tolerate it, Nick decided with grim determination. If by some chance he and Desiree were able to pursue a normal relationship after this business with Ron was finished and they did make love, he'd just have to make sure that when they were finished, she wouldn't have the strength to give him the heave-ho, much less the necessary energy to pick up a pen. Feeling somewhat smug, Nick smiled blandly and absently scratched his chest.

"Why don't we go back up to my room?" she suggested. "We can order room service and uh, get started."

Nick nodded. "Sure."

"Great. We'll start with the pleasure enhancers and save the, uh, more adventurous toys for tomorrow."

Nick mentally scowled at that remark. She made it sound as though he couldn't handle the "adventurous" toys. Admittedly, the whole idea of sex toys was distasteful to him, but that was a personal choice, not the result of a weak sense of adventure. He could be every bit as adventurous as the next guy.

"Don't hold back on my account," he told her.

She cocked a brow, regarded him with a secret smile. "You're sure?"

"Yes," he said, slightly exasperated.

"Fine. We'll start with the vibrators."

# 5

―――――

WHILE NICK HAD stepped next door to return a call, Meg took the time to retrieve her journal and arrange the many boxes of adult toys/enhancers on her bed. She sorted by category. Vibrators, massagers, enhancers, various creams, jellies and massage oils, a few bondage items and adult games.

In just a few minutes, Nick would join her and she would be required to do a little Show and Tell session on each individual item. The idea simultaneously inspired a rush of panic and a tingly coil of anticipation. Her insides quivered.

*He* made her insides quiver.

Meg couldn't begin to explain, much less rationalize the profound relief of seeing him on the other side of her door this evening. She'd grinned stupidly and a long, quiet sigh had slipped past her lips. The tight knot of tension that had sat like a stone in her belly had magically dissolved, leaving her calm and irrationally pleased. And all the while, like a heady background noise, the ever-present insistent thrum of awareness zipped along her ultra-sensitive nerve endings.

She still couldn't believe that he'd agreed to pre-

tend to be her lover for Mr. Kent's benefit. Frankly—
excellent kisser aside—he just didn't seem the type.
Didn't quite fit the profile. Nonetheless, Meg had
never been one to look a gift horse in the mouth.
She'd summoned the nerve and asked, he'd said yes.
End of story.

Besides, since she'd started critiquing these toys,
meeting people associated with the business, she'd
learned to put expectations aside.

For instance, a little white-haired grandmotherly-
looking type had approached her this morning and
thanked Meg for her helpful critique on Oriental
Nympho Cream. She'd been right, the old lady told
her in a quavery falsetto. It did indeed make a
woman have multiple orgasms. The old woman had
smiled benignly and shuffled off with her big patent-
leather purse clutched in the crook of her arm.

Stunned, Meg had suffered a TMI moment—Too
Much Information. Before she could stop it, a horrific
image of the old woman in the throes of passion had
manifested in her mind's eye. Meg had resisted the
dramatic urge to clasp her hands over her face and
scream, "My eyes! My eyes!"

A few minutes later, she'd seen the elderly lady
again, this time fondling a dildo. The woman had
peered at it through her bifocal lenses, passed it back
and forth between her hands, turned it this way and
that in the same fashion she might have used to select
a nice piece of fruit. Meg shook her head in wonder.
You just never knew about people.

Case in point, just because Nick didn't seem like

he'd be the type to play a sex-toy critic's lover didn't mean that he couldn't be one. Granted, he was sexy. When he'd gazed at her through those heavy-lidded eyes and told her that he was "intensely attracted" to her, Meg had melted with pleasure, with need. She'd sensed a subtle change in him, almost like she'd unwittingly sprung a trap; he'd put her in the crosshairs and moved in for the kill.

There had been something distinctly predatory hidden in that sleepy gaze, Meg realized now. Another mini-earthquake quivered through her belly.

Still, Meg thought, no matter how sexy he was, something about the role he'd agreed to play didn't quite fit him. She chewed her bottom lip. She couldn't exactly put her finger on it, but she intuitively felt it all the same.

Nick rapped lightly on the open door frame. "Hey."

Meg grinned. "Come on in."

God, he was gorgeous. He wore a pair of navy slacks and a white oxford shirt open at the throat. In deference to the late-summer heat, he'd rolled up the cuffs, revealing tanned muscular forearms lightly dusted with golden hair. A designer watch circled his wrist.

Despite the smile, Meg concluded his call hadn't been a pleasant one. His gilded tawny curls were a bit mussed, as though he'd plowed a hand through them repeatedly in frustration, and the smile, while sincere, seemed a little tight around the edges. Tension didn't radiate off him, just sort of hovered around him like a shadow he couldn't shake. It was a subtle difference, but one she noted quite clearly.

Meg considered asking him if everything was okay, but decided against the idea. It was none of her business. If he wanted her to know what was wrong, he'd tell her.

Oh, to hell with that, Meg decided. "Is something wrong?" she asked, unable to help herself.

"Nah. Just a small glitch with a client." He shoved his hands into his pockets and strolled toward the smorgasbord of sex toys piled on top of her bed. His eyes bugged. He blinked in astonishment and whistled low. "My God." His gaze swung to hers. "Y-you, uh, play with all of this stuff?"

Meg chuckled. "Not play—critique," she corrected. "There's a difference."

He aimed a sexy grin in her direction. "I realize I'm not the expert here, but don't you have to play to critique?"

"Not always," Meg replied, feeling her toes curl at the innuendo loaded into that statement. What she wouldn't give to play with him. "There are some things that I'm not into—like bondage—so I just do the best that I can with what I have to work with. I still try to determine whether something's a good product or not. If I'm not sure, I just say so."

"Not into bondage, eh?" He tsked regretfully. "There goes that fantasy. Why not?"

Unable to tell if he was serious or joking, Meg ignored the fantasy remark and considered the question instead. "Trust," Meg replied after a moment of quiet contemplation. "Bondage requires a great deal of trust."

Though she hadn't been restrained during the college fiasco—hell, Grant hadn't even taken the time to remove his pants, much less put any thought into being original—Meg certainly felt as if she had. The old familiar hurt and frustration welled, but Meg battled them aside. People could be bonded without the actual restraints in place. Deceit and mistrust could hold a person back far more effectively if the hurt were great enough.

Deciding turnabout was fair play, Meg managed a strained smile and fired the question right back at him. "What about you? Are you into bondage?"

He lifted a shoulder and one corner of his mouth tucked into an endearing grin. "Never tried it."

"Then that makes two of us."

"So." He rocked back on his heels. "Where do we start?" he asked.

"I thought we'd start with dinner. Is that okay with you?"

"Sure. We can save the sex for dessert."

Suddenly a picture of her slowly nibbling her way down his splendidly muscled chest rose in her wayward mind. Something hot and dark and needy unfurled low in Meg's belly and settled in her sex. Her eyes strayed to the chest in question, to the tender yet masculine side of his neck. To where his pulse beat strongly beneath the golden skin. Meg longed to taste him there, to feel the methodical *thump*

*thump thump* of his life force flowing through his veins. She swallowed tightly.

God, she just *wanted.*

Unable to form a reply, Meg manufactured a slightly brittle grin. "Let's order room service."

A knowing twinkle flickered in his gaze. His lips curved into a slow, thoroughly sexy smile. "Sure."

Meg retrieved the menu from the bureau and offered him a seat at the small round-topped table in the corner of the room. Once they made their selections, Meg called downstairs and placed the order. "They said it would be around thirty minutes," she told him as she replaced the receiver.

Nick didn't seem to be able to keep his gaze from straying to the bed. Meg saw him look from item to item, saw his golden gaze alternately narrow, widen, blink. He seemed morbidly fascinated, like someone who'd passed an accident on the freeway and couldn't stop gawking.

"Would you like to go ahead and get started while we're waiting on dinner?" she asked.

"Uh...sure." Nick shrugged his shoulders like a prizefighter before stepping into the ring. Cracked his knuckles. "I'm ready."

"Ohhh-kay." Meg laughed. Taking pity on him she said, "Look, I was only kidding downstairs about the vibrators. We can start with something else if you're uncomfortable with those. Most straight men aren't into them. They're, uh, primarily a woman's toy."

He flexed comically again. "I can handle it."

"Okay, then." Meg stood, crossed to the bed and scooped up several of the long, phallic instruments and spread them out on the table. She forced the tremor from her fingers as she picked up the smooth red seven-inch first. "This one is called the, uh, Red Devil," Meg said. "It requires two size-C batteries and has three variable speeds. For a more realistic feel, you can add a jelly sleeve like so—" Meg expertly smoothed the cover, complete with head and vein-like ridges, upon the vibrator. Her gaze met his. "Obvious use aside, vibrators can be used for more than vaginal stimulation. Erotic massage, for instance. Any questions?"

He looked utterly and completely astounded. He swallowed. Stared at where her fingers rested on the authentic-looking penis. A muscle ticked in his tense jaw and he shifted uncomfortably in his chair. "No."

Moving right along then, Meg thought. She picked up the next one. It was a flesh-toned seven-inch. "This one is called Cupid's Arrow. As you can see, no jelly sleeve is required." Meg gestured to the side of the vibrator. "A-and it's very life-like."

"Right," Nick said grimly, nodding. "That one has nuts."

Startled, Meg almost dropped the vibrator. "Right. It does have, er, testicles. It, too, requires two C batteries and has three variable speeds."

"Oh, do tell," Nick said in a dramatic game-show voice. "Does it come with a handy carrying case as well?"

Meg smirked. "No."

He pulled a disappointed face. "Bummer."

Meg gave him a hard stare, tried but failed to flatten her lips. She picked up the ten-inch black. "This one is called the Ebony Avenger," Meg told him. She gestured to the enormous realistic-looking penis. "This one requires two D-size batteries—"

"D's, huh?" He whistled low.

"Yes, D's. It has four variable speeds—"

"But no nuts."

Meg strangled on a laugh. "Correct. No...nuts."

Finally, Meg picked up the last of the full-size vibrators. This one was a multi-talented wonder and Meg couldn't wait to see the look on his face when she turned it on. "This one is called The Stud. In addition to having three variable speeds—" Meg turned it on and the head of the vibrator began to swivel "—this one has a rotating tip."

He grunted. Shifted in his seat.

"The testicles on this one are filled with soft silk beads which rotate as well." Meg flipped another switch. She held it below the head as both ends of the toy came to life. Smiling, she shrugged. "Double the pleasure, double the fun."

"That's— That's...interesting," he managed at last.

He didn't look interested, Meg noted. He looked comically disoriented. That slumberous gaze of his took on a glazed look. She took pity on him and turned if off. "That, uh, takes care of the vibrators."

"Thank God," he muttered under his breath. He

passed a hand over his face. Fidgeted in his seat. "What's next?"

A knock sounded at the door. Meg grinned. "Dinner."

*DAMN!* NICK THOUGHT as he signed for the bill. If he had to watch Desiree manhandle one more fake erection he'd have a friggin' stroke!

Nick concentrated on controlling his breathing, on slowing down his racing pulse. He was generally unflappable, could make himself remain calm. His job alone required that he be able to don a mask of sorts. Keep a cool head. He could hardly be an effective attorney if he couldn't keep an impassive face.

But this week... This harebrained scheme had all but shattered his usually stalwart fortitude. By week's end, he'd undoubtedly need a little padded room devoid of sharp objects. Nick didn't recognize himself. This lust-crazed, perpetually aroused basketcase wasn't him.

*She'd* done this to him.

Nick glanced accusingly at the woman in question. Desiree swiftly transferred their dinner onto the table—to his immediate relief, she'd removed the vibrators. That sleeveless gauzy dress clung to her curves, outlined the swell of her breasts. Her arms were long and graceful and she moved with an internal rhythm, an innate elegance.

The glow from the floor lamp illuminated the side of her face, casting the other side in shadow. Her silky shoulder-length curls shone with health, with a natural color that wasn't the result of a talented stylist. Her jaw was smooth, strangely vulnerable, yet with a tilt that suggested she could be stubborn when the mood suited her. Nick felt a grin tug at his lips. A peculiar emotion swelled in his throat, forcing him to swallow.

Watching those petite capable hands gliding over those incredibly lifelike rods had been utter torture. Nick had tried to make light of the situation. Had tried to be funny.

But inside, he'd been writhing in agony.

Batteries, variable speeds and all that nonsense aside, he hadn't been able to keep from imagining her hands on *his* rod. Palming him, stroking him, gliding over the head of his penis.

Then he'd taken the vision one step further and imagined that sinfully carnal mouth of hers subjecting him to the same torturous ecstasy. Her lips, her tongue, stroking him, licking him, sucking him until he shuddered with the force of his climax.

If she could do this to him while talking about the vibrators—which he found unequivocally repulsive—what in the hell would happen to him when they moved on to some of the other things displayed on her bed?

Admittedly, Nick was a novice when it came to sex toys. He'd never used any, had never required any to service a woman and they had no place in his black-and-white world. Quite frankly, that swiveling wiener she'd held up last had shocked the shit out of him. Nick had never imagined that such things existed, or better still, that anyone would use such a gadget.

But at least he'd known what it was. For the most part, Nick could tell what most of the things were, or at the very least their general purpose. He'd spotted some edible underwear—that was pretty self-explanatory. Something called Tickle Dust with a long pink feather. Nick assumed you feathered the stuff over your partner and licked it off. His gaze once again returned to Desiree. Heat rushed to his loins. He could get into that.

But there were at least a couple of things that Nick couldn't even begin to fathom what they were, much less used for.

Those were the things that gave him pause. Made him nervous. They probably needed to save those toys for tomorrow night, Nick decided. He simply didn't think he could withstand any more sexual stimulation tonight without some form of relief. His poor penis had been suffering the fiery torment of the damned for the past thirty minutes while she matter-of-factly fondled those vibrators.

He simply couldn't take anymore.

He'd lost control—again—and Nick never permitted himself to lose control.

They'd enjoy dinner, then he'd return to his own room and subject himself to a cold shower.

"Are you ready to eat?" she asked.

Nick nodded, somewhat mollified with a plan of action and strolled across the room—he refused to look at the bed—then took his seat across from her. "This looks good."

Desiree's pert nose wrinkled slightly. "It'll do."

In the process of taking up his knife, Nick paused. "What? Is something wrong with yours?"

A rosy flush stained her cheeks and she smiled self-consciously. "Uh, no." She nudged a bit of wilted parsley to the side of her plate. "I'm just very picky about my food. Presentation, especially." She gazed at her entrée with a hint of disgust. "It's a pet peeve of mine. It's silly."

Frankly, Nick had never cared about the presentation of his food. So long as it was edible, he didn't care what it looked like. Still, however mundane, this was a personal preference not pertaining to sex and he knew so little—other than what she permitted him to know—about her. Perhaps this conversation would lead to a more telling one.

"Okay. I'm curious." He gestured to her plate. "What's wrong with the way your food looks?"

She raised a skeptical brow. "Are you serious?"

"Certainly." He sipped his wine. "Enlighten me."

Her pleased grin caused his chest to swell, momentarily giving his male equipment a much-needed break.

"Well." She swallowed and gestured to her entrée with her fork. "This plate has no harmony."

"No harmony?" Nick repeated.

"Right. Think of a clock face. The steamed vegetables—obviously not fresh or they would be crisp instead of limp—are scattered from ten to two. The roll—which could double as a hockey puck—is sitting between four and eight where the meat traditionally belongs, though some chefs are going to a more stacked presentation. Still…" She shrugged. "This is pitiful. I'm only a pastry chef and I know better. This would never leave my kitchen." Her gaze met his. "An empty plate is a chef's canvas, where she displays her art—and cooking is an art." She tsked. "Whoever prepared this has absolutely no pride in their work. No passion for the process."

Nick gazed at his own plate and noticed that his steak hadn't been properly positioned either. The rather unappetizing grilled rib-eye sat at nine o'clock on his plate. From now on, Nick realized, this would drive him nuts. Every time he looked at his plate, he'd be checking the position of his food—and he'd think of her.

Desiree cut into her chicken, completely oblivious to the life-altering little bomb she'd just set off. "Generally speaking, when a chef pays as little attention to presentation as this, he's going to have put the same halfhearted attention in the preparation." She took a bite and nodded. "Yep, I was right. Glad we didn't order dessert." She snorted. "I've got stuff on my bed that tastes better than this."

"Don't eat it," Nick blurted.

She looked startled. "What?"

"Let's go somewhere. Out to eat." Nick didn't know where this was coming from, but he went with it all the same. It felt right. Getting her out of here—

out of her room with all those toys mocking him from the bed—seemed like the right thing to do.

"You want to go out to eat? Tonight?"

"Yes."

A slow smile flipped her frown into a heart-stoppingly gorgeous smile. She nodded once. "Okay."

Nick tossed his napkin into his plate and stood. "I'll call and have the valet pull my car around while you get your purse."

"Okay."

Nick met Desiree by the door. "You pick where we go. You're the expert."

"So you've said." She sighed as she gazed up at him.

"Well, you are." Nick paused and traced a half-moon on her smooth cheek. "You're every man's fantasy. You know your food and your sex." He smiled. "If you're an armchair quarterback as well, I'm in trouble."

She returned his grin, thankful for once that her father had drilled the sport into her practically since birth. "How does it feel to be in trouble?"

"Dunno," he said huskily. "But I bet it tastes good."

Though he knew he shouldn't, knew where it would lead, Nick lowered his mouth to hers. An intense mind-numbing heat swept him from head to toe as her sweet tongue tangled with his. Blood rushed to his groin, stiffened to the point of pain. Dammit. Kissing her would never be enough.

Nick heaved an internal sigh. Regrettably, it would have to be.

He had to preserve some part of his honor, and taking advantage of her by sleeping with her was simply out of the question. Desiree didn't know why he was here, didn't realize that she'd essentially brought the enemy into her camp. She was simply a beautiful, vibrant woman acting on instinct. She had no idea that Nick had ulterior motives for befriending her, that if she wasn't who she claimed to be, he'd be responsible for getting her fired from *Foreplay.*

No matter how desperately he might want to, he could not sleep with her.

The thought rang with more futility and less conviction than Nick would have preferred.

# 6

MEG DIDN'T KNOW what had prompted Nick's invitation to go out to dinner, her critique of the room service perhaps. Whatever the reason, she found herself secretly pleased at the impromptu request.

Now came the tricky part—picking a fine restaurant in Atlanta where she wouldn't be recognized by either an owner or a chef.

For all intents and purposes, for the rest of the week, she was Desiree Moon. In order to truly delve into that character, Meg couldn't risk Nick finding out her true identity. She wanted to simply be Desiree for the next few days and then just disappear.

Furthermore, though chances were slim of Nick inadvertently letting her critiquing job slip in front of someone who really knew her, that was also a chance she didn't want to take. Renauld was a fanatic about appearances and would consider Meg's *Foreplay* job horribly scandalous. Though she'd been nothing but an asset to him for the last four years, he still nevertheless wouldn't hesitate to fire her.

So where could they go?

Fine cuisine was a specialized business, resulting in a small, intimate circle of competitors. Restaurant owners made it a point to know the competition—to learn the reputations of the chefs at competing restaurants. The information they gleaned served them in several capacities. It kept the menus fresh and up-to-date, it indicated trends in service and customer relations, and occasionally, it led to offers of employment for a particularly talented chef.

Meg had had several such offers during her four years of service at *Chez Renauld's*. She'd always refused. She'd been part of a team that had literally put *Chez Renauld's* on the Who's Who list of haute cuisine. She'd created her niche at the intimate restaurant and had no intentions of leaving.

Ever. All the more reason why she had to be so careful.

Once she had Pierre's course under her belt, she'd be one of the top pastry chefs in all of Atlanta. She'd be on her way to truly establishing herself in a splendidly specialized art of cuisine.

Her adamant refusal to play the rotating game—despite staggering incentives—had earned her unparalleled recognition among her peers. As such, she knew most everyone associated with the business—and they knew her.

Getting out of a restaurant without having someone blow her cover to Nick would be next to impossible.

Her gaze strayed to where Nick's fingers rested on the steering wheel. His hands were beautiful. Big and square with long, surprisingly graceful fingers. Meg remembered the feel of them skimming her ribs, kneading her rump. Imagined them dancing up her spine, leisurely tracing the seam of her panties, slipping between her legs... Warmth cascaded through her, fizzed up her thighs.

Yes, getting out of the restaurant without having someone reveal her identity to Nick would be next to impossible—but unquestionably worth the risk.

"So," Nick said, "where are we headed?"

"Have you ever been to *The Matador?*"

Nick shook his head. "I've heard of it, seems like my partner has taken clients there, but I've never had the pleasure. Is that where you'd like to go?"

Meg nodded.

Nick cocked his head in her direction, smiled one of those intimate come-hither smiles of his that turned Meg's insides to pudding. "Then *The Matador* it is."

Nick seemed more relaxed, Meg noted. Less troubled, for lack of a better description. The taut lines she'd noticed around his mouth had eased and he appeared to be more confident with each mile they put between themselves and the hotel.

Poor Nick, Meg thought. Though she'd tried to warn him, he obviously hadn't been able to truly grasp what would be required of him in his role as her critique partner. Seeing all those vibrators, all those sex toys, had apparently been too much for his Insert Tab A into Slot B mentality. He'd seemed fine for a while—eager even, before they'd gone up to her room—but as the lesson had progressed, as she'd proceeded from one vibrator to another, Nick had become increasingly agitated. Uncomfortable.

Obviously, Nick had let his attraction for her propel him into a situation he didn't quite know how to deal with and he was too much of a gentleman to back out. Meg knew she should let him off the hook. Knew that she should come up with an alternate plan.

But she desperately wanted to play. With him.

She wanted to explore every sensual possibility and she couldn't dream of asking for a better partner.

Besides, adult toys were meant to be only that. Toys. Primarily for couples to enhance their sexual relationship. While it was true that some single adults used them for other recreational purposes, they weren't designed to take the place of a partner. More so to complement that partner, to enhance their sexual experience together.

That's what she wanted to show Nick, to do with him. Learn, experience, play.

True, she was practically a virgin. She had more experience with adult toys than with men.

But something told Meg that this was a lesson Nick Devereau desperately needed to learn. Somehow, before this week was over, before they returned to their normal lives—a pang of regret struck her at the thought—she'd make him understand that things weren't always as black and white as he believed. Some things could only be seen in shades of gray. That would be her gift to him for going along with this scheme, for helping her with Marcus Kent.

She'd help him see the grays.

WHY ON EARTH had he thought taking her out of the hotel—specifically, out of the bedroom—would help him regain control?

Clearly, Nick had deluded himself.

During the twenty-minute drive to the restaurant, he had managed to convince himself that getting Desiree into neutral territory would somehow give him the upper hand. Put him back into the driver's seat, so to speak. He'd be protected from her beguiling charm, wouldn't find her as sexy. He mentally snorted. Nick had actually believed that he'd regained control of this situation. After all, he was supposed to be all but seducing her—not the other way around.

Just over an hour later he knew the truth.

He'd been wrong. So totally wrong.

He'd simply traded one form of torture for another. Watching her fondle sex toys had been a cakewalk next to this.

Watching this woman eat had to be the single most erotic thing he'd ever witnessed.

Desiree didn't simply eat—she savored every bite, every aspect of the meal. She'd requested a secluded table near the back, ordered the wine and then asked Nick if he would do her the honor of letting her order for him. Nick had agreed and had to admit, she had exquisite taste. Though he'd been exceedingly distracted during the course of their dinner, his meal had been delicious.

Desiree popped a cherry tomato into her mouth and groaned with pleasure. Her pink, facile tongue darted out and captured a drop of creamy Parmesan sauce from the corner of her lip. Her eyes fluttered dreamily. "Mmmm. This is heavenly."

Yeah. Whatever, Nick thought. If she didn't keep that clever little tongue of hers in her mouth, the strength of his erection would upend the table.

She took up her glass and slowly sipped her wine, regarding him above the rim of the flute. Her eyes held a sated, dreamy quality Nick found every bit as arousing as watching her eat. He imagined she'd look like that when she came.

"How's yours?" she asked.

"Excellent," Nick managed.

Her bottom lip glistened with leftover wine. The pool of candlelight centered in their table cast a golden glow over the vibrant tone of her smooth skin. God, she was gorgeous. Art in motion, and completely clueless as to how utterly captivating she was.

For instance, she couldn't possibly know that at this very minute she was in extreme danger of having her rear planted in his lap, having that sexy little dress hiked up to her waist. This act would coincide with the swift elimination of her panties and the swifter addition of himself buried into her heat.

Nick set his teeth so hard he feared they'd crack. If he didn't regain some semblance of control—and soon—he'd undoubtedly embarrass himself by exploding in his pants like a randy teenager in the middle of a wet dream.

Nick braced himself as she took up her utensils again. He stared as she expertly carved a small piece of chicken from the breast on her plate, tracked the slow progress of the morsel to her mouth.

Watched the fork disappear between her lips.

Watched it slide back out.

To his immense discomfort, she moaned again, a little mewl of pleasure that sent another rush of heat straight to his crotch. He twitched again, felt his erection straining against his pants.

She took her time chewing the bite, obviously relishing each individual spice as it caressed her palate. She swallowed, causing the delicate muscles in her throat to work in a sensually intriguing pattern.

Nick looked at her plate. More than half of her meal remained. He wouldn't make it. Couldn't.

"I can't get over how hungry I am," she said, smiling. She glanced at his plate and noticed the majority of his entrée still remained. A line emerged between her delicate brows. "Are you finished?"

"Er, no," Nick said. Actually, he'd been too distracted to eat his meal—one appetite had been replaced with another. Still, maybe if he concentrated on eating his own food, he wouldn't be so preoccupied with how she consumed hers.

"Good," she enthused. "Because they make the most wonderful desserts here. Their pastry chef is particularly talented with chocolate. He makes this Raspberry Chocolate Dream that is to die for." She shuddered, purred with pleasure. "Mmmm. I can't wait."

His sex wept a single tear of desire in warning. Bloody hell.

Nick tossed back the rest of his drink in a single gulp. Dove into his remaining meal with gusto. She chuckled softly, drawing his attention.

"So you do like it," she said. "I was afraid you were only humoring me."

"No. It's excellent," he admitted. "The best steak I've ever had. I've just been too busy watching you to enjoy it." The confession slipped out before he could check it.

She lowered her lashes, blushed. "Watching me? Why?"

"Do you do everything like this?" Nick asked, curious about this facet of her personality, despite the hard-on. "So wholeheartedly?"

She mulled it over. Absently stroked the stem of her glass. "I guess so. What's the point of doing something unless you do it wholeheartedly?"

It was a good philosophy, Nick thought, but he'd never met anyone who actually succeeded in applying it to their life. What other things did she do? he wondered. What other aspects of her life received such unqualified attention to detail?

For the first time since he'd started this mission of mercy for his brother, Nick wondered if Desiree had someone waiting for her at home. Someone whom she loved…wholeheartedly.

For reasons he couldn't explain, call it a sixth sense or whatever, Nick just knew that wasn't the case. If some lucky bastard owned her heart, was the recipient of her wholehearted affections, she wouldn't be wasting her time with him. She didn't seem capable of the duplicity, Nick decided.

Which made him wonder again why he was even here. If she weren't capable of duplicity, then why had he picked up on a couple of little inconsistencies that lent credence to Ron's theory? Like Antonio, for instance. If there really was an Antonio—and Nick truly believed the man was nothing more than a figment of her imagination—then where was he? Why wasn't he here? How was she critiquing the partner-oriented toys when she evidently had no partner? Things simply didn't add up and Nick needed more information before he could make an educated assessment.

After this week, he'd probably never see her again, Nick realized. He didn't know why, but he intuitively knew that Desiree had no intention of giving him her real name. She didn't want him to have it. She'd had the opportunity to give him her real name the first day they'd met and she hadn't even hesitated when she'd said Desiree Moon. Hadn't turned a hair at the lie.

This woman had an agenda of her own for this week and for whatever reason, it didn't involve her being anyone but her alter ego. This week she was Desiree Moon and that was all she planned to show him. Nick knew it as well as he knew his own name. True, he might slide a few questions under her radar, might glean a few personal insights. She might even invite him into her bed. But she wasn't going to give him anything she didn't want to.

Nick could wrestle her for control all he wanted, but he grimly suspected it wouldn't do any good.

She was the one in control.

And the hell of it was, she didn't appear to even know it.

Desiree licked her lips once more. That slow flicker of her tongue was all it took to put him at the bursting point again. She expelled a soft, satisfied sigh. "That was scrumptious. Do you have room for dessert?"

Not if you asked his pecker, Nick thought. "Sure."

"I'm too full to eat a whole portion by myself. Why don't we share that Chocolate Raspberry Dream I told you about?"

Nick nodded. "Sounds great."

Actually, Nick would rather have his testicles removed with red-hot pincers than share a dessert with her because he knew that he wouldn't survive the experience without embarrassing himself. But he couldn't tell her that, now could he?

Nick ordered the dessert and asked for two spoons. It was delivered in short order. It was one of the prettiest dishes he'd ever seen, and he recalled Desiree's comment about the plate being a chef's canvas. That was certainly the case with this particular confection. It could have graced the cover of a magazine.

Chocolate sauce had been drizzled around the plate, cocoa sprinkled haphazardly around the edges. In the middle of the dish sat an ultra-moist dark chocolate square of cake topped with a light chocolate mousse. Two chocolate wafers had been positioned on top and a single raspberry crowned the dessert. Chocolate shavings and two mint leaves completed the look.

"Isn't it pleasing to look at?" Desiree asked. "*This* dish has harmony." She loaded a spoon and held it up to him. "Here, try a bite."

Oh. This wasn't a good idea. In fact, this was a really bad idea. "I, uh—"

"Go ahead," she urged. "You do like chocolate, right?"

Nick's throat constricted. "Yeah."

"Well." She gestured with the spoon. "Go ahead. Open up."

Nick reluctantly opened his mouth and allowed her to feed him. The chocolate taste melted onto his tongue, the varying textures from the cake, mousse and thin wafers mesmerized the senses. It was dark and rich and unequivocally the best-tasting dessert he'd ever put into his mouth. Nick was surprised when he heard a moan and realized it had come from his own throat. "It's wonderful," he murmured thickly.

Desiree chuckled. Delight sparkled in those gorgeous mossy-green eyes and her smile struck a chord in him that resulted in another tidal wave of lust. "I'm glad you like it."

She loaded the spoon again—the spoon she'd just fed him with—and lifted it to that unbelievably sensuous mouth. The morsel disappeared as her lips closed around it. Her eyes fluttered shut, and another orgasmic groan vibrated from deep in her throat. It was intimate and erotic and simply more than he could bear. Her tongue snaked out. She licked the spoon.

Nick shot up from the table. "Excuse me."

Desiree's startled gaze swung to his. "Ok—"

"I'll be back in a moment."

It took ten to walk it off and when he returned he felt like the biggest ass that had ever walked the earth. She'd pushed the plate away, disappointed and obviously bewildered at his abrupt departure. The smile he'd grown so accustomed to seeing seemed a little too bright, more manufactured than real. The sparkle had died from her eyes and a dejected slump rounded her small shoulders. He swallowed. His fault, Nick realized.

He couldn't take that.

"I have a confession to make," Nick said softly.

"Oh?"

Too bright, but he gave her credit for trying. She'd been giving him her wholehearted attention all night. Much more than he deserved. He'd inadvertently hurt her feelings, yet she still seemed determined to give him the benefit of the doubt.

"I know I've acted a little strange tonight, but there's a perfectly logical explanation."

"There is?"

Nick blew out a breath. "Yes. I'm in lust with you."

The confession made a smile tremble around her lips. "You're in lust with me?"

"Yes," Nick confessed, oddly relieved. "I have been since the moment I first saw you. You're gorgeous and you're interesting, and you make me laugh and you have the sexiest mouth I have ever seen—" He leveled his gaze on hers. "I've been sitting here watching you eat—just eat, dammit—and the whole time I've been battling a hard-on. When you ate off my spoon just now— Licked the spoon—" Nick looked away, blew out another breath. "I had to get up. Do you understand?"

Her brows winged up her forehead. "Are you saying—"

"I'm saying *I had to get up,*" he repeated meaningfully.

A calculating grin turned her lips. "Or what?"

The minx. She was determined to drag the words out of him. He supposed he owed her that much. Nick passed a hand over his face. Managed an embarrassed smile. "Or I would have left the restaurant with a wet spot on the front of my slacks."

"Oh." She looked disappointed.

Oh? That was it? She'd made him all but tell her that he'd been hard all evening long, had practically exploded in his shorts and all she had to say was "oh" punctuated by a pout? "Was that not what you were expecting me to say?" he asked.

"Frankly, no."

"No?"

"No," she repeated.

"Then what were you expecting me to say?"

She arched a brow. "Frankly?"

"Yes," Nick said, growing exasperated. "Frankly."

"Well, frankly, I expected you to say that watching me eat turned you on so much that you almost came. That every time I put that fork in my mouth you were imagining putting something else between my lips. Like your..." Desiree leaned forward and whispered the rest of the words in the most erotically graphic, depraved, sensual monologue Nick had ever heard.

Dear God, she was killing him.

Nick's breath came in short, hard puffs. He gripped the side of his chair with both hands and a bead of sweat broke out on his forehead. To his immense pain/pleasure, Desiree's toes snaked up the side of his leg, brushed his inner thigh, and settled on his groin.

Nick exploded. He came. Hard.

Desiree smiled. Calmly slid the dessert from the middle of the table and took up her spoon. She moaned, groaned, wriggled and wiggled, all the while licking and laving that utensil.

Her foot remained anchored at his crotch.

Her clever toes nuzzled and stroked, and didn't let up until she'd finished her dessert and he'd considerably enlarged the wet spot on his slacks.

So much for control.

By the time they left the restaurant Nick had reached a grim realization—being honorable with a

woman hell-bent on seduction was a damn diffi-
cult task.

Yes, Desiree had her own agenda, and after that
little toe-session underneath the tablecloth, Nick
knew exactly what she wanted.

Him.

# 7

"THANKS SO MUCH for doing that workshop," Ann told Meg as they walked out of the Colorado Room. "I think the vendors really benefited from your lecture."

Meg wasn't so sure, but she thanked her for the compliment all the same.

There'd been one guy in the back who'd stared at her through the entire session, watched her every move and hung on to her every word. He hadn't frightened her. It hadn't been that kind of look. This guy had been younger than most of the men and women present and he'd seemed particularly interested in her opinions.

To Meg's surprise, there'd been something oddly familiar about him, but she couldn't imagine why. She was certain she'd never met him before. Most likely, he'd been a recipient of one of her bad reviews. She hadn't given many and certainly hadn't ever given one to a product that didn't deserve it. In fact, most of them had been with the same company.

Something clicked in Meg's troubled thoughts. She stopped. "Ann, who was the younger guy in the back? The one who asked so many questions?"

Ann's pert nose wrinkled. "Brown hair, heavy on the gel?"

Meg nodded. "Yeah, that's the one."

"Ron Capshaw," she drawled. "Fancies himself a ladies' man and is prone to brag." She shrugged. "Seems oily to me but Marcus says he's a good guy, just needs to grow up. Marcus is usually a good judge of character."

The name didn't ring a bell, but that didn't mean anything. She racked her brain, searching for the connection. "What company is he with?"

"He owns—"

"Guilty Pleasures, Inc." Meg finished, as the name she'd been searching for finally materialized. "That explains it."

"Explains what?" Ann asked.

"Why he glared at me through the whole session." Meg bit her lip. "I've given several of his products bad reviews."

"Did they deserve them?"

"Oh, yeah," Meg readily agreed.

"Then you have absolutely nothing to feel guilty about. You've been doing your job. That's all." Ann firmed her chin. "He needs to take your advice and make the adjustments to his product line. I'll say something to Marcus."

"No," Meg insisted. "Don't do that. It's not a big deal. I'll just ignore him."

And hope that he ignored her. She had at least three Guilty Pleasure products upstairs right now awaiting her critique. She certainly didn't plan to let him intimidate her into a favorable review if the stuff didn't deserve the praise. Still, if they weren't up to par, this could get seriously uncomfortable.

Luckily, Meg had a protector this week.

Nick.

Just the thought of him made her shiver.

Dinner last night had been an experience. Meg still couldn't get over how bold she'd been, how forward. A slow smile curved her lips.

But he'd deserved it.

Meg hadn't had any idea that he'd been sexually excited, that *that* had been his problem. He'd seemed strained, tense throughout their meal, but she'd just glumly assumed it was because he regretted asking her out. That she'd talked too much about their food—Meg was passionate about her work, loved to talk about it—and had turned him off with her continual chatter. It wouldn't have been the first time.

Still, she usually wasn't so dense. Last night had apparently been an off-night for her.

But once Nick had confessed, once he'd explained his preoccupation… Well, everything had gone from being clear as mud to clear as glass. And something had come over her. She'd gone into full Desiree mode.

She'd been so relieved, so bowled-over by his I'm-in-lust-with-you statement that her blood had instantly caught fire. That admission had tripped her naughty wire and ignited a wicked bomb.

She'd talked dirty to him.

Said exactly what she wanted to say in just the

way she wanted to say it. Hadn't held back. She'd put her foot between his legs, massaged him to climax twice—in a public restaurant. It had been nothing short of a breakthrough, Meg marveled. Nothing short of miraculous. For her.

Aside from that one little moment of panic when Chef Roberto Villarreal had started to make his rounds, the night couldn't have been any better. Meg frowned, chewed her nail. She knew Nick had noticed her discomfort when she'd spotted the chef. She'd all but leapt from her chair, hastily excused herself to the ladies room. She'd taken the long, circuitous route in order to bypass Villarreal. Then, she'd stayed hidden in the bathroom for a ridiculous amount of time.

But she'd had to. She and Roberto had attended a seminar together in June, barely four months ago. They were more than acquaintances; they were friends. She'd hoped that he would have made his rounds earlier in the night, but she hadn't been so lucky. Just par for the course, Meg silently lamented, her typical run-of-the-mill luck.

Still, though she knew he'd noticed, Nick hadn't commented on her abrupt departure. And he wouldn't, she knew, because he wasn't the type. He was... He was honorable, Meg decided. The term was old-fashioned and outdated, but it applied to him. Perhaps that was why she didn't have as many reservations with him, why she'd been blown away by the full force of her attraction. The misgivings she normally felt when presented with a potential partner had been absent from the get-go with Nick. They hadn't been there to act as a filter against the attraction. Without that safeguard in place, she'd been able to experience the blunt force of her need.

"By the way," Ann said, drawing Meg's attention back to the here and now. "Mr. Kent wanted to see if Wednesday evening would be all right to have that dinner meeting?"

Earlier than she would have liked, but it would do. That would leave her one more night to prep Nick for their performance. "Sure. That'll be fine."

"Seven o'clock in Mr. Kent's suite okay with you?"

Meg nodded. "Sounds lovely."

"Great." Ann beamed. "I've gotta run. See you tomorrow night."

Meg took a bolstering breath and checked her watch. She and Nick were meeting again tonight to finish up his lessons. They'd need to go over her journal, and finish up with the other toys in her room.

Speaking of which, Meg thought, she needed to critique a few items before he arrived this evening, and upload her reviews onto the Web site. If she didn't take care of the majority of the products before she left this week, she'd never get caught up once she got home. It was now or never. Resigned to that end, Meg made her way back to her room.

"HAVE YOU MADE any progress with her yet? Learned anything useful?"

"It depends on what you mean by useful," Nick

said. He thumbed through the paper, idly scanned the sports page, though he wasn't really reading it. He needed to call his mother, make one more attempt to try and talk her into investing her retirement fund and was trying to frame his argument in his mind before he presented her with the idea again.

Ron huffed an exasperated sigh, clearly annoyed at Nick's evasive comment. He sat at his desk, booted up his laptop. "Has she let anything slip? Does she have a partner?"

Nick sighed, growing more uncomfortable with his role in this farce by the minute. "I told you last night, things have taken a bizarre turn. I'm playing the part of her sex-toy critique partner, remember?"

"Yeah, and that's strange. Why does she need you to pretend to be her lover? If she had one, why didn't he come with her?"

Nick had wondered that himself, but he didn't want to add any fuel to his brother's fire. "Marcus Kent didn't see her liplocked with someone else in the hall—he saw her liplocked with me. She needed *me* to play the part."

"If she'd brought Antonio, she wouldn't have needed you at all," Ron pointed out stubbornly. "This is all we need. I say we go with it. Out her for the fraud she is."

Irritation rose. "It's not enough, Ron. Before we ruin this woman's career we're going to be certain that you're right. It's not enough," Nick repeated adamantly.

"But she didn't bring a lover! That should tell you—"

"If she'd brought a lover," Nick growled through clenched teeth, "my getting close to her would not be necessary. You'd know beyond a shadow of doubt that she wasn't a fraud."

Which was the only reason Nick had gone on with this ridiculous farce. She'd completely undone him last night. He'd lost it. Remarkably, twice—a phenomenon in itself. In the middle of a five-star restaurant. She'd turned him into someone he didn't even recognize, was dragging him into unknown emotional territory. Nick didn't like it. Didn't know how to deal with it.

Regrettably, the head with the brain wasn't leading this expedition.

"Do *you* think she's a fraud?" Ron asked finally.

Nick sighed. He honestly didn't know. True enough, she'd propelled him to orgasm twice—with her feet, of all things. But he'd been sitting there with a hard-on, ready to rip his hair out, for chrissakes, and she hadn't recognized the signs. It just didn't add up. He couldn't make the pieces fit. "I don't know," Nick admitted after a moment. "But I doubt it."

Ron shrugged. "Maybe I should call Mom."

A red mist swam before Nick's eyes. "Like hell, little brother. I agreed to go along with this scheme, and I won't go back on my word." He paused, pinned Ron to the chair with his gaze. "But if she's not a fraud—if she's the genuine article—then you'll correct the problem with your product line on your own. You will not ask Mom. For anything. Not for one red cent.'' It wasn't a statement, or even a command. It was a warning. "It's time that you take some responsibility for your actions.''

"What do you think I'm trying to do?'' Ron shot back, facing his computer once more. "I've put everything I've got into this business and I can make it work. I know I can. But I can't do it if she keeps giving me those horrible reviews.'' Ron paused as he stroked a few keys on the on the computer. "I saw her today.''

Nick looked up. "So, you saw her. What was the problem?''

"She's just so damn smug, Nick.'' Ron sighed dejectedly. "Like she knows everything. And I'm telling you, she doesn't *know* anything. Mark my words, when this week is over you'll have to admit that I'm right. I'm right about this one,'' he insisted desperately.

"Have you even considered that she might know what she's talking about? That it might behoove you to make improvements to your product line?''

Ron rolled his eyes so far back in his head, Nick was certain he must see the roots of his hair. "No offense, but you don't know anything about the adult-toy industry. There's nothing wrong with my products.'' He sniffed, but wouldn't meet Nick's gaze. "She just has it in for me.''

Nick felt tension begin to knot in his neck. "Ron, that's absurd. She doesn't even know you. How could—''

"Sonofabitch!" Ron muttered hotly.

"What?"

"She's done it again. Dammit." Ron gestured wearily at the screen. "Look at this. Ah, hell." He speared his fingers through his hair. "Did she have to do this now? At the damned trade show? Couldn't she have at least waited until she got home to post this load of bull?" Ron turned back to Nick. He jabbed a finger at him. "This is your fault."

"My fault?" Nick repeated, astounded.

"You were supposed to stay close to her," Ron ranted. "Keep her occupied. If you'd been doing what you agreed to do, she wouldn't have had time to write this damned review."

"I can't keep an eye on her twenty-four seven," Nick returned. "Furthermore, she's just doing her job."

"Yeah, how 'bout you doing yours?" Ron retorted. "The quicker we can put her out of commission, the better. What time are you supposed to meet her tonight?"

"Six," Nick said tightly.

"Don't leave her side." He turned pleading eyes to Nick. "You've got to take care of this. She's ruining me, Nick. This one will work. I know it." He sighed, rubbed the bridge of his nose. "I get so tired of being the family failure, so tired of always letting you and Mom down. Dad died before I could make him proud of me. Hell, all you ever had to do was breathe and you had his approval. Why couldn't he have shared even a little of it with me? Was I so hard to love?'' Ron asked quietly, once again re-minding Nick of the painful, unfair truth. "Help me make this one work. Please."

Nick sighed. "I'll do what I can."

"That's all I'm asking for."

NICK LEFT his brother's room and headed to the bank of elevators at the end of the hall. The tension that had begun at the back of his neck had spread to his shoulders and down the middle of his back. A ball of unease sat and festered in the pit of his belly.

Nick gave a sigh of frustration. He felt like he'd been hijacked by a nightmare, trapped in a bad dream and didn't have a prayer of waking up to put an end to the madness.

How had things escalated to this point? Nick wondered. How had things gotten so completely out of control? He'd simply been trying to spare his mother more heartache, help her hang on to his father's hard-earned money. His intentions had been honorable, despite the dishonorable method he'd been forced to employ.

But from the moment he'd started this damned ruse, nothing had gone according to plan. Every time he tried to regain control, to keep his perspective, Desiree threw him a curve ball. Rewrote the script. Nick kept telling himself that the new playbook she handed him would work to his advantage, but he grimly suspected he was only deluding himself.

Nick Devereau had never had any reason to delude

himself. The perceived weakness made him ball his hands into fists, made him itch to punch something.

Nick prided himself on being logical, on staying one step ahead of the game. Right now, he didn't know where he stood—didn't even know if he was still in the game, for that matter—and it simply drove him crazy. Hell, he didn't want to be here, didn't want to be doing Ron's dirty work.

And he especially didn't want to hurt Desiree.

But he couldn't help Ron without essentially destroying her. He swore hotly. That had been fine in theory, when he'd simply been looking at an abstract picture. When he'd only had his mother's feelings to contend with.

But now the whole sordid scenario made him feel petty and small and left him with a bad taste in his mouth.

Because he knew her.

True, he didn't know her name. But he knew the smell of her perfume, knew that she was thorough and obsessive when it came to her work. Knew that she hummed when she didn't think anyone was listening and that she sometimes laughed so hard she cried. She had a wicked sense of humor, was hot for him and could make him hot by simply breathing.

No, by God, he didn't know her name—but he knew enough about her to know that he didn't want to hurt her. He knew that her Desiree Moon alter ego was very important to her. Nick didn't know why. Didn't understand the significance. Hell, maybe she found her real self lacking in some way. He couldn't imagine why, but knew that women sometimes got their wires crossed when they held a mirror up to themselves.

Nick didn't claim to know all the mysteries of the female mind—heaven forbid. He certainly didn't know everything in Desiree's head.

But he wanted to.

And that's what had sent him into a tailspin. That's what scared the living hell out of him. He shouldn't want to know those things about her. It didn't factor into his mission, into the damned job he'd come here to do. The more he learned about her, the harder it would be to set her up for the fall.

If Ron were right about her, Nick would have to pass the information along to Ron. He had no choice. It would be the right thing to do, and Nick Devereau always did the right thing. Cut and dried.

But the more time he spent with her, the less right it felt.

Nick passed a hand over his face, loosened his shoulders and forced himself to calm down before he knocked on her door. Despite his present turmoil—despite it all—he couldn't wait to see her.

How messed up was that?

Desiree pulled the door open and a smile bloomed on his lips. She grabbed his shirt, yanked him inside and laid one hell of a kiss on him. Breathing hard, she pulled back. Happiness and desire sparkled in those gorgeous green eyes. "I've been thinking about you," she said huskily.

Just like that, every trouble he'd carried with him

from Ron's room melted away. Nick felt a smile tug at his lips. Something warm and pleasant ballooned in his chest. "You have?"

She nodded. "I have."

"What exactly have you been thinking about?"

She tilted her head up and offered her mouth again. "Kissing you…and stuff."

Bloody damn. "And stuff?"

She nuzzled his neck. "Lotsa stuff."

"Hmmm," Nick hummed. That sounded promising.

"But—" she sighed "—I suppose we should get business over with first. Marcus Kent wants us to have dinner with him tomorrow night."

"Is that going to be a problem?" Nick asked.

"No, not really. But there's still quite a bit of inventory we need to cover." Desiree threaded her fingers through his and led him deeper into the room. "When we're finished, though, I wondered if you'd hang around and watch a movie with me. That new Denzel Washington film is on pay-per-view."

That sounded great, Nick thought. They could lounge around, watch a movie and relax. He desperately needed to relax. "Sure. That sounds great."

Her tentative smile brightened. "Excellent. Do you mind if I finish with a couple of reviews before we get started?"

"No." Nick shoved his hands in his pockets. "Do whatever you need to do."

"Thanks."

Nick noticed that she'd cleared the bed, had trans-

ferred all of the rest of the toys and such to boxes
that lined the walls. Her laptop sat on the small table
they'd shared the night before. Everything was neat
and tidy, organized. A small floral-bound book lay
open beside the computer. The dreaded journal, Nick
surmised.

Desiree sat cross-legged in the chair. She'd twisted
her curly hair up into some sort of clawlike thing and
a few chocolaty tendrils clung to her neck. Today
she wore a pair of white capri pants with a bright-
yellow sleeveless tank top. She'd left the sandals off
and those talented toes had hot-pink nails. Her feet
should come with warning labels, Nick thought, recalling what those dazzling little digits had done to
him last night.

"Have you worked a lot today?" he asked.

"Uh, a little. I had to give a workshop this afternoon." She frowned as her fingers flew across the
keys. "Had one guy sort of heckle me."

Nick frowned. Amazingly, anger blindsided him.
"Heckle you?"

"Yeah. This guy named Ron Capshaw. He owns
Guilty Pleasures, one of the companies I critique for.
I've given his products a few bad reviews. He's taken
it personally, it seems. Jerk," Desiree humphed.
"It's not my fault that his line's not up to par."

*Damn.* What had Ron been thinking to call attention to himself like that? Thank God he'd decided to
spare their mother any future humiliation and used
his middle name—Capshaw—as his last for business
purposes. Still, heckling Desiree in the middle of that

workshop was the height of stupidity. Nick mentally swore. He could cheerfully throttle his brother right now, Nick thought darkly.

"He's not gonna like it," Desiree continued, "but I added a couple more today. Bad product, bad review." Her chin firmed adorably. "I'm not going to be intimidated by anyone."

"Did, uh— Did he say anything to you?" Nick asked. He'd kill him if he did, Nick decided. Brother or no, he'd simply be forced to kick his ass.

"Not directly, just asked me a bunch of stupid questions." She shook her head. "It was weird. He kept staring at me like he knew something I didn't. It was bizarre." She shrugged it off.

"So what was wrong with the products?" Nick asked as casually as he could.

"See for yourself," Desiree told him, still preoccupied with her review. "They're in the box closest to my bed. It's the edible undies and the lubricating gel. The undies taste like stale licorice and the gel could double for axel grease." Her nose wrinkled. "It's third-rate all the way."

Nick imagined she was telling the truth, but wanted to see for himself. He picked up the edible underwear first—hell, at least he'd heard of these. This stuff had been around for years. He'd even eaten a few pair.

He took one bite and promptly spat it back out. Nasty!

Desiree laughed at him. "I warned you."

One bite of those underwear would wilt the

staunchest erection, Nick thought, attempting to dredge the taste by swallowing repeatedly. Given the choice, he'd drink sour milk before he'd put those rotten underwear back in his mouth.

Though it was probably a waste of time, Nick uncapped the lubricating gel and forced a small amount from the tube onto his finger. The thick, dark brown substance looked suspiciously like it had leaked from a soiled diaper. Nick sniffed it, recoiled. It also smelled like something that had leaked out of a soiled diaper. Reluctantly, Nick rubbed it around on his fingers. It was gross, felt sticky and slimy. Given the intimate nature of this particular product, Nick couldn't imagine any good purpose it could possibly serve.

He sighed.

She was right—Ron's products sucked.

# 8

---

"THIS IS A penis jelly ring." Meg tossed the small nubby ring to Nick for his inspection, then crossed the room to get a couple of canned sodas from the minibar. "That's the thing that Mr. Kent asked you about out in the hall. Remember?"

He grinned ruefully. Scrubbed a hand over his face. "I'm trying to forget."

"Yeah, well. Not yet." Meg plopped his drink down in front of him and settled back into her seat. "I don't care if you get permanent amnesia after tomorrow night, but you've got to have a mind like a steel trap until then." Meg grinned. "Do you have any questions?"

"Yeah. What the hell does that thing do? What's it for?"

"Well." Meg swallowed nervously. "First, uh, depending on a man's size, you have to soak it in hot water, stretch it to fit." Meg did her best to ignore Nick's dubious expression. "Then you roll it onto an erect penis until it fits snug at the base. It acts like a tourniquet of sorts, prevents the blood from receding after climax and subsequently results in a longer erection."

Nick grunted. Scowled. "Why are those little knots all over it?" He gestured to the pile on the table. "All over all of this stuff, for that matter?"

Heat scalded Meg's cheeks. "The, uh, soft nubby texture acts as a clitoral stimulator."

"Come again?"

"For the woman," Meg explained. "A clitoral stimulator. And, in some cases, a vaginal wall stimulator."

Nick's expression turned pained. A muscle ticked in his tense jaw. "Let's move it along, shall we?" he said in a slightly strangled voice. "What's next?"

"I'll let you pick."

He shrugged and randomly picked up a small tube. "What's this?"

"That's called Virgin Again. Once applied, it makes the muscles which line the vaginal walls, uh, tighten. Contract, for that first-time-feel all over again."

Nick's brows shot up and he examined the tube with interest. "Well, what do you know? Does it work?"

"Dunno."

His gaze found hers. "Haven't critiqued this one yet, huh?"

"No, not yet," Meg lied. That would be one of those items she'd simply have to BS her way through. She'd need a male perspective for that particular product and considering she didn't have one, it would be next to impossible to tell if the cream actually worked.

"What about this?" Nick asked, peering intently at another product he'd selected from the table. He stretched the elastic bands like a slingshot. "What does this do?"

Laughing, Meg snatched it from his fingers. "This is called a Hummingbird."

"Doesn't look like any bird I've ever seen," Nick commented dryly.

"Be that as it may," Meg replied, "this is actually a neat little toy." Meg held up the elastic bands, stretched it out so that Nick could see how the toy was supposed to fit. "These bands fasten around a woman's hips and the bird nests, literally, between her legs."

Nick's mouth went slack.

"It's the same principle as a jock strap," Meg explained, growing warm. "See?"

He nodded, still seemingly paralyzed.

"This little gadget requires two double-A batteries, has three variable speeds and comes with a handy remote. Theoretically, a woman could strap this baby on beneath her clothes, trip the remote from her pocket and pleasure herself…anywhere. At a board meeting, in the car, strolling down the aisle of a grocery store. Amazing, isn't it?"

Nick swallowed. "Have, uh— Have you used one of those?"

"I've critiqued similar products," Meg admitted as a rush of heat spread through her limbs.

"A-are you wearing one now?" he asked hoarsely.

She chuckled. "No."

"Thank God," Nick breathed fervently. He closed his eyes. Opened them. Closed them again. "Okay. We can move on."

"Are you sure?"

He nodded, apparently unable to form the necessary word.

Meg showed him a pair of fuzzy handcuffs. "Self-explanatory."

He nodded. "So if you've never used them, how do you critique them?"

"Well, first I check to see if the lock opens properly, doesn't stick. I make sure that the craftsmanship is quality, not second-rate. Then I check for comfort. I manacle one wrist like so—" Meg fastened one of the cuffs on her hand "—then I make sure that it's not painful, that the padding around the cuff is sufficient. Make sure that it doesn't chafe." She inserted the key into the lock and released the cuff. Her gaze met his. "That sort of thing."

"So, you've never let your real critique partner handcuff you?" Nick asked casually. Too casually.

"No," Meg replied as she sorted through the various articles on the table. It wasn't a lie per se— she'd never let *anyone* handcuff her.

Nick quirked a perceptive brow. "That trust issue again?"

"That's right," Meg murmured. After Grant—

The Big-Mouth Two-Minute Wonder—she couldn't imagine surrendering that kind of power to anyone. After a moment, she said as much. "That act requires more submission than my character was formed to permit. It's not just a trust issue, though that's certainly a huge factor. It's the yielding of control to another person." She managed a self-deprecating smile. "I'm not very good at that."

Nick returned her grin. A unique understanding simmered in his caramel gaze and something else, something she couldn't readily identify. "Me either," he admitted. He expelled a breath. "So what's next?"

Meg sipped her soda. "You tell me."

"Okay." Nick took a sip of soda and perused the table once more and picked up a small black and gold package, similar to a jeweler's box. "What's this?"

"Ben Wa Balls."

Nick choked on his drink. His eyes watered. "Ben-*what* balls?" he wheezed.

Smothering a chuckle, Meg bit the side of her bottom lip. She quickly removed the box from his hand, flipped the case open and swiveled it around so that he could see. Twin silver balls, slightly smaller than walnuts, gleamed from inside the case. "Ben Wa Balls," she repeated slowly.

Clearly, Nick didn't have a clue what these were used for and, judging by his equally perplexed and horrified expression, his imagination appeared happy to oblige with all sorts of scandalous and depraved possibilities for their use. He passed a hand over his face, rubbed the back of his neck. "Do I really need to know what these are for?"

"I suppose not," Meg replied, avoiding his gaze. She flattened her twitching lips.

Nick saw her mouth quiver. His eyes widened accusingly. "Go ahead and laugh at me," he said, half-chuckling now himself. "This is new territory for me. I'd managed to go my entire adult life without knowing about any of this stuff." He motioned impatiently with his hand. "Virgin Again and vibrators with rotating tips and that Bird-thing—" His eyes narrowed. "From now on every time I look at a woman, I'm going to wonder if she's got one of those strapped on beneath her clothes. Wonder if she's on the brink of—" He blew out a breath, forcing a calm he didn't feel. "But I can see that you're dying to tell me about those damn balls, so go ahead," he offered magnanimously. He chuckled. "I think I'm past the shock point now."

Meg sincerely doubted it, but she wouldn't tell him that. She was relatively familiar with all aspects of the adult-toy world and she still found herself routinely shocked.

After all, she hadn't shown him any of the gay and lesbian toys. He'd have a stroke if she pulled out that double dildo the Man-To-Man company had sent her last month. Or the oral sex machine. Or the blow-up dolls. The list went on and on.

But the Ben Wa Balls were harmless. He could handle them.

Meg cleared her throat. "Are you certain?"

"Yes."

"Okay. The Ben Wa Balls are an exercise tool for a woman. They're like little dumbbells for the vaginal muscles."

"Is that right?" Nick cocked a brow. "Do they come with a workout video?"

"Very cute." Meg smirked. "Anyway, a woman inserts them into—"

"I know where they go," Nick interrupted tightly, his voice taking on an uncharacteristic high-pitched tone. "How do they stay there? What keeps— What keeps them from falling out?"

"That's where the muscle part comes in. They're excellent for strengthening the—"

"The muscles. Right. I got it. Let's move on."

He didn't look ready to move on, Meg noted. He looked ready to bolt. She resisted the urge to park herself in his lap. To wrap her arms around his neck and flatten her breasts against his powerful chest.

A wry grin twisted her lips. After last night's behavior, that certainly wouldn't shock him. She still couldn't believe that forward siren who'd massaged him to climax with her toes and talked dirty to him was her. She never did things like that…never behaved so boldly. It was fun being Desiree Moon. Meg had never felt so free, so completely liberated and alive.

Presently her body thrummed with heightened awareness, with an insistent need that bordered on frantic. Meg had watched Nick run his hands through his hair, repeatedly mussing the tawny locks. His tanned skin was slightly flushed, and she longed to kiss the grimness from his beautifully sculpted lips, watch those butterscotch orbs darken with desire. Warmth burned the tops of her thighs, flowed determinedly toward her feminine core.

Meg took a shallow breath, summoned composure. They had to finish this first, she told herself, willing her erratic pulse to slow. Keeping her position with *Foreplay*—making Paris a reality instead of a dream—depended on Nick's performance. If she couldn't get the deer-in-the-headlights look off his face in the privacy of her room, she didn't have a prayer of him pulling off the necessary performance in front of Marcus and Ann. A finger of apprehension tripped down her spine. She couldn't even think about the ramifications of failure. It simply wasn't an option. She needed the job, needed the money and the future financial security it could give her.

"Uh, Nick?" Meg began hesitantly.

"Yeah?"

"Do you know something I don't?"

He snorted dubiously. "I doubt it."

A giggle bubbled up into her throat. Poor Nick. He thought she had all this experience, that she was some sort of sex guru. Little did he know, she thought with a silent sigh. "No, I mean...is there some sort of catastrophe about to strike? A fire? Tornado? Earthquake?"

His brow furrowed. "Er…no. No, not that I know of. Why?"

"Because you look like you're waiting for a root canal without anesthesia. Braced for impact."

"I'm not braced," he denied, straightening a bit. "I'm, uh…just concentrating very hard." He delivered the line deadpan, but ruined it when his eyes began to crinkle in the corners. Then he outright laughed.

Mercy, Meg liked that laugh. It vibrated deep inside her. "Well, just make sure when you concentrate very hard tomorrow night that you do it with a smile. The brooding, horrified mask you're wearing now isn't very convincing as a merry sex-toy critic."

That heavy-lidded gaze found and held hers. "But tomorrow night, I just won't be playing the part of the merry sex-toy critic—I'll be playing the part of your lover." The last word was uttered as a caress and Meg felt it all the way to her little toes. "Trust me, that's a part I'll be able to play without any problem whatsoever."

A warm tingle started at her scalp and shimmied down. Gooseflesh broke out on her arms and she quelled a shiver. "Well," she said for lack of anything better.

"What's next?" he asked, releasing her from that mesmerizing stare.

Meg blinked. It took a good five seconds to recover from the lust-induced hypnosis Nick had wound around her. She glanced around the table, forced herself to focus. "Just a few more things here, then you'll need to review my journal. You can take a look at it sometime tomorrow, if you'd like."

Nick nodded. "That would probably work best. Let's finish up here and then settle in and watch that movie you mentioned."

"Okay." She poked her tongue in her cheek, and surveyed what was left on the table that they hadn't covered. To her surprise, she'd inadvertently saved her three favorite things. She took up the first one, a small mini-massager. "This is called the Baby Bullet," Meg told him. "It has a variable speed remote control and is largely used as a clitoral stimulator." She grinned. "But it can also be used for intimate massage." Meg placed the small massager into a soft nubby glove and tripped the remote. "Hold out your arm," she told Nick.

"I, uh—"

"For heaven's sake, it's just your arm. It's not like I told you to drop your pants," she told him with an exasperated huff.

Nick grudgingly held out his arm. Meg gently stroked the strong muscles of his extended limb. Ran the pulsating glove back and forth, circle upon circle. He blinked, seemingly startled at the pleasant sensation. A slow smile bowed his lips. "That's... nice," he said, skeptically surprised.

Meg quirked a grin. "Yeah, just imagine how it feels against your back or against your neck. Your thighs, or gliding up the insides of your calves.

I-it's very relaxing.'' Meg had to turn it off—she was becoming too turned on. A fleeting frown passed over Nick's handsome face as she withdrew the glove.

"Well, at least I understand the significance of all the little knots on everything now,'' Nick said with a self-deprecating grin. "Damn, that felt good.''

"Did, didn't it?'' Meg agreed, pleased that he'd admitted to enjoying the massager.

Nick studied the table with a new appreciation of sensory pleasures. He certainly wasn't a kid in a candy store, Meg conceded, but the change was almost as drastic. He seemed genuinely intrigued now.

"What else have you got here?''

Meg selected another favorite. "This is Shiver Cream.''

"Shiver Cream? Sounds interesting. Do tell,'' he murmured silkily.

Meg uncapped the lid and loaded her finger with the almost colorless cream. "Give me your arm again.''

To Meg's delight, this time he didn't even hesitate. She cupped his hand and applied the cream to the inside of his wrist. "Now wait just a minute,'' she said. "Feel anything?'' she asked.

"Nah, not really.'' Disappointment tinged his voice. "Am I supposed to?''

The secret smile she'd barely managed to keep

hidden, curled her lips. Meg lowered her lips and blew lightly on his wrist.

Nick's eyes widened and he whistled low. Shuddered. "Damn. I-it's hot and tingly. What did you call this stuff again?"

"Shiver Cream. Like it?"

"Yeah," he breathed. "Blow me again."

Meg's startled gaze flew to his and a wicked chuckle erupted from Nick's throat. Her blood caught fire at the Freudian slip, simmered in her veins as graphic images tumbled one right after another through the secret cinema of her mind.

"Blow on my wrist again," Nick clarified, that slumberous gaze unwavering.

Meg lowered her lashes, bent low and zigzagged a steady stream of air against his sensitized wrist. Nick inhaled sharply, his breath hissing through his teeth. Meg felt her breasts go heavy, her nipples bud. A ribbon of warmth threaded through her and settled in her womb. She ached for release...ached for *him*.

"Th-that's incredible." Nick sighed.

"I like it," Meg admitted.

That somnolent gaze once again captured hers. Something dark and sinful and slightly mischievous lingered there. "Want me to do you?"

The ground shifted beneath Meg's feet as another lust-quake detonated below her navel. Her breath trembled through her lips. A vision of those gorgeous lips hovered centimeters above her flesh gripped her, made her mouth parch with want. *Say yes!* a little voice screamed inside her head. *Say yes!* One word and he'd do it. Just one word. *Say yes!*

"Yes," Meg finally managed, and she smiled at the coup. Advantage Desiree.

Nick tugged her into his lap and Meg settled willingly, nervously, but ready to be led. "Now, where should I put this?" Nick mused softly, his voice low and rough and full of promise. "Ah, I know." Huskier this time, deeper.

He pulled her hair from her neck and tucked it over her shoulder, then painted a trail from behind her ear down the side of her neck. His touch alone created a sizzling trail of sensation. He nuzzled her neck and blew softly.

The swift tingly heat made her shudder. A purr of pleasure vibrated the back of her throat.

She felt his smile against her skin. "Like that, do you?"

"Y-yes." Meg sighed shakily. "Blow me again."

Nick tensed, and a husky moan rumbled from between his lips. He sent another wave of warm air over her neck, making her shiver. Then, to Meg's immediate melt-down, his lips replaced his breath. Slow, sweet nibbles, the lave of his tongue against her sensitive skin. She was coming unglued. Her limbs had liquefied and a low insistent throb had commenced between her burning thighs. Meg clenched her feminine muscles, felt the slick heat coat her folds. Need and want coalesced into something primal, something just out of her reach and out of her control.

He had control, Meg realized. He was hot, he was ready and he wanted her, but he held back—she could feel it. He'd somehow managed to cast her into the writhing pit of sexual hell, while he'd kept himself in check. How had he managed to—

"Do you remember what you did to me last night?" Nick asked huskily.

Meg couldn't reply, simply nodded.

"Remember how you set me off? Twice. Made me come in my briefs?"

His tongue swirled around the shell of her ear. She nodded again as scenes as thrillingly graphic as his words materialized behind her closed lids.

"I'm going to do that to you now," Nick promised, or warned, she couldn't tell. "I'm going to hold you and make you beg and set you off— twice."

Nick tilted her jaw toward him and kissed her, lightly at first, then put his complete intent into the erotic caress and laid siege to her mouth. He swallowed her groan, threaded his strong fingers into her hair and angled her more firmly against him. She felt him harden against her rump, felt the full length of him rub a few scant inches from that part of her that longed for that part of him. Meg wiggled in his lap. Frowned through a kiss despite the persistent flow of pleasure cascading through her body.

She wanted— She needed— Meg turned in his lap, straddled him. Her sex nestled above his, provided that sublimely carnal pressure she craved. Smiling now, she framed his face with her hands, explored his mouth more fully and pressed herself tightly against his magnificent chest. Her nipples pearled beneath her bra, rasped against the silky fabric.

As though she had telegraphed her needs, Nick slid his hands under her top and deftly released the hook of her bra. Those talented hands skimmed her rib cage, then trekked slowly upward until he held both aching globes in his hands. He squeezed and tweaked, thumbed and palmed her, and all the while, his lips never left hers. His tongue thrust in and out of her mouth, mimicking a rhythm that had unconsciously begun below their waists. He rocked slowly against her mound, wreaking havoc everywhere. Her mouth, her breasts, her sex.

A coil of heat tightened low in her tummy. Meg felt her breath start to come in short little puffs. She whimpered against his mouth and he upped the tempo. Barely, but enough. Her skin dewed, became flushed. A frantic beat pulsed where her pelvis met his.

Nick released her breasts, smoothed his hands down her body and finally anchored them at her hips. The climax she'd craved hovered just out of her reach. She could feel it there, ready to starburst and eddy through her. But she couldn't reach it, she couldn't—

She wanted—

She needed—

Nick sucked hard at her tongue, held her firmly and rocked even harder against her. Once, twice...Meg's body bowed with shock as release swept her up in a tornado of sensation, then she shuddered violently. A moan tore from her throat and she sagged against Nick's chest as the aftermath of the climax pulsed through her. Her eyes fluttered shut and a contented sigh whispered past her lips.

"More amazing than I'd ever dreamed," she murmured, wonder in her voice.

Nick's breathing was still labored, but growing steady. He gently stroked her back and kissed the top of her head. "One down and one to go."

# 9

A RING OF THE PHONE reluctantly propelled Desiree from Nick's lap. He missed her warmth at once. Nick had never held a more responsive woman. Had never enjoyed a partner's climax more. Her little pants of pleasure, that soft satisfied purr that had resonated from deep in her throat all but sent him over the edge. The only reason he'd been able to hold it together was that he'd been so intent on taking care of her, so determined to send her where she'd sent him last night.

Completely over the edge.

She'd gone, all right. Gone and sent a postcard to taunt him. She'd shattered, had acted as though she'd never had the pleasure of an orgasm in her life. But of course, he knew better. He need only look around the room, check out her arsenal of sex toys to know that she'd been on the receiving end of countless orgasms. He had heard the relentless buzz of the vibrator. She'd just done a convincing job of making him feel like the first man to ever take her there, making him feel special.

Nick watched her from across the room. Her skin still held that fresh-from-pleasure island glow. Her lips were swollen from his kisses and a becoming flush stained the side of her neck that had received the most of his attention.

Shiver Cream, indeed, Nick thought, absently scratching his chest. That was some potent stuff. Nick had been stunned to realize that he'd liked it, hadn't expected to enjoy any of these so-called adult toys. But the sensation had been hedonistic, surprisingly erotic. Once she'd applied it to him, he'd been consumed with thoughts of applying it to her...all over. Then fanning his breath over every square inch of her. Licking her. One thought had triggered another until he'd finally snapped and pulled her into his lap.

A feral grin claimed his lips. He couldn't wait to do it again.

Desiree ended her call. "That was Marcus Kent," she told him, looking slightly disappointed and annoyed. "One of the vendors is leaving and he'd like me to come down and say goodbye. I hate to do this, but do you mind if I run downstairs for a moment?"

Nick shrugged. "No, of course not."

Relief lightened her shoulders. "Why don't you read through my journal while I'm gone?" she suggested. She reached behind her back and refastened her bra. Absently straightened the rest of her clothes. Thirty seconds later, she'd pulled her hair up in that claw-clip again, glossed her lips and shoved her feet into her sandals. She moved through the room like a whirlwind with a purpose. Nick had never seen a woman get it together so quickly.

If she was self-conscious, or even mildly disconcerted about their recent love-play, she certainly didn't show it.

He found himself equally impressed and irritated.

After that little stunt she'd pulled at the restaurant last night, he'd had to wait a solid fifteen minutes before he could walk. She'd left his lap as pretty as you please in less than two minutes and looked fresh and chipper, as though they'd shared a cappuccino— not a mind-blowing, back-clawing orgasm.

He was being unreasonable, Nick told himself, feeling his jaw clench painfully. What difference did it make if she could recover more quickly than him? It didn't lessen the impact of what they had shared.

He'd just made her come, for chrissakes.

He was The Man, Nick silently affirmed. He couldn't imagine where this Neanderthal mentality was coming from, but he didn't seem able to stop it. It would certainly account for the absurd urge he'd had to beat his chest and roar after she'd collapsed against him, sated and spent and thoroughly pleasured.

Desiree handed him her journal, bent down and pressed a quick but meticulous kiss to his lips. "I'll be back," she promised.

And he'd have her on her back, Nick thought.

Bloody hell. Another oafish thought. Nick shut his eyes, rubbed the back of his neck. A soft whoosh sounded as the door closed silently behind her. With nothing else to do, he turned his attention to the journal.

Nick didn't readily open it, just traced a finger down the spine. Strangely, he found himself reluctant to read it. This innocuous little book held the potential to ultimately finish what he'd come here to do. Though he truly believed that Desiree didn't have a lover, the possibility still existed and the proof could very well lurk in these pages. If that was so, he'd be done here. Finished. He'd be able to report his findings to Ron—Ron would be furious, of course—but Nick would be able to go home and return to his life.

Incredibly, the idea of returning to his plush, sterile condo in a trendy new complex here in Atlanta didn't instill the profound relief he'd fully expected to feel. A peculiar, almost hollow feeling settled in his gut. Nick took a sip of his warm soda, chalked the disconcerting sensation up to hunger.

He couldn't possibly be depressed at the thought of going home, of quitting this insane charade.

Nick had a life, a career waiting on him, after all. He typically worked a twelve-hour day, then spent an hour or so at the gym to burn off the stress he'd accumulated in the office. After he left the gym, he'd call one of his favorite eateries—the numbers were efficiently programmed into the address book in his cell phone—swing by, grab dinner and relax in front of the TV until he fell asleep. At some point, he'd wake up, stagger to bed, and then start the whole process over again each morning. He certainly didn't live life in the fast lane, but there was a certain comfort in the routine. Or so he liked to think.

After a few moments, Nick mastered his emotions,

took a deep, resigned breath and stoically opened the
journal. Desiree's neat script filled the lined pages.
She'd dated each entry, recorded the name of the toy,
the company who produced it and her first impressions after use. If he had to choose three terms to
describe her work, the words, neat, professional and
organized would aptly sum it up.

This woman didn't do anything halfway, Nick
thought with a small grin. Absolutely nothing. A kernel of respect grew for her. He'd bet his time-share
that she alphabetized her spices, color-coded her coat
hangers and bought her plastic bins in bulk. She
probably kept every bank statement, every tax form
and could put her hands on her insurance policies in
less than ten seconds. She seemed to thrive on order
and didn't allow any unnecessary clutter in her life.
If he was wrong and she did have a lover, Nick concluded grimly, he'd undoubtedly be a husband soon.

Only a fool would let her go.

With that telling thought, Nick steered his attention to a more productive task—reading the journal.
Nick had scanned enough briefs in his career to sift
through the details and retain the pertinent facts. He
put that talent to work and when he was finished,
blew out a ridiculously relieved breath—no lover.
He'd been right.

Which meant that Ron could very well be right
also. His brother's bizarre theory started to almost
seem plausible. Could she actually be doing all of
this solo? Granted, there were some products she
didn't necessarily need a partner for. That damned

bird-thing, Nick recalled with a surge of irritation. Some of the creams and jellies.

But what about all the other stuff? Nick wondered. What about the penis jelly rings and the handcuffs and the adult games? What did she do about those things? Make it up?

Surely not, Nick mentally scoffed. Still, a niggle of doubt surfaced. Dirty talk and talented toes aside, all the data pointed to Ron's theory. Nick took a moment to examine the facts. One, she hadn't brought anyone with her. Two, she hadn't admitted to having a significant other who might have tested these toys with her. And three, there was no mention of him—Antonio—in her journal. Furthermore, Nick had spent a great deal of time with her, had been in her room for the past couple of nights and she hadn't received one personal phone call. Every call had been trade-show related.

Pretty damning evidence, he decided.

Nick swallowed. Swore. What a damn mess. It was a no-win situation. Either Desiree lost her job or his mother lost more of her retirement. And though he'd come here to help Ron, Nick knew he couldn't permit either scenario to happen. Desiree didn't deserve to lose her job for the sake of Ron's shoddy products, and his mother simply couldn't afford to bail him out again. Nick would simply have to find another alternative. A fraud or no, Desiree's assessments of Ron's products were right on the money. Ron had simply needed a scapegoat, but Nick couldn't allow him to use Desiree.

Nick exhaled loudly and, for lack of anything better to do, glanced around Desiree's room. Everything was neat and tidy. No clothes littered the bed or floor, having obviously been stowed in the appropriate space. Various bottles of female paraphernalia lined the low dresser and a nice attaché and matching handbag sat on the floor beside the bed. All in all, everything was just as he'd expect her to—

Nick stilled as everything inside him went quiet. Her handbag...which undoubtedly held her driver's license.

One glance would tell him her real name.

Elation surged through him. The opportunity was too good to pass up. Nick stood quickly, ignoring the nervous flutter that had begun in his stomach as well as his squawking conscience. He hurried to the door, slowly pulled it open and peered out into the hall. Empty. Even if she were in the elevator, she'd still have to come down the hall.

He had time.

Nick double-timed it back to the bed and picked up her purse. His conscience had begun to screech in protest now, almost drowning out all of his legitimate reasons for snooping through her personal possessions.

Ah, hell, Nick silently argued with himself. He frowned as indecision tore at him. His hand hesitated on the zipper. This would probably be his only chance. What if she didn't tell him her real name? What if she left, walked out of his life forever, and he had no way of ever finding out who she was?

If she wanted you to know, she'd tell you, his mean-spirited, smart-assed conscience argued reasonably.

Shit. Nick couldn't argue with reason. With a defeated sigh, he set her purse back down, careful to make sure that he placed it right where he'd found it.

The phone rang. Before it occurred to him that this was Desiree's line and she might not want him to answer it, Nick had already lifted the receiver and uttered a greeting.

"What's she doing downstairs?" Ron hissed angrily. "I thought I told you to keep an eye on her. I swear, Nick, you are really blowing this. If you don't—"

Nick blinked. "Have you lost your mind?" he bit out, glancing nervously toward the door. He set a hand at his waist. "Why are you calling me on her phone?"

"Her phone?" Ron repeated blankly. "I dialed your room."

"No, you didn't. This is Desiree's room, you idiot!"

"Well, I guess it's a good thing you answered it," Ron replied, as though this mistake couldn't have been potentially disastrous. Couldn't have ruined everything up to this point. "From here on out, you're going to have to shadow her. You can't let her put one more bad review on that Web site. What's she doing downstairs without you?" Ron wanted to know.

"She had to go down and tell someone goodbye," Nick growled. "Look, Ron. Your plan won't work and I'm having to improvise here. Just give me some time."

"What do you mean my plan won't work?" Ron asked. "I've told you I know she doesn't have the experience to critique. If she doesn't have the experience, then she shouldn't be doing the job."

"Whether or not she has any experience doesn't change the fact that your products suck, Ron. I tried them. They're awful."

"They don't—" Ron began.

"Yes, they do," Nick insisted. "Instead of worrying about the reviews, you need to be worrying about improving your products. Making changes that will benefit—"

"I can't do that without funds, big brother, and if I go bankrupt as a result of her reviews, there won't be a product line to improve." Ron paused. "She has got to be stopped. Bottom line. Make it happen."

The line went dead.

MEG BADE Mr. Liggett of Bedroom Fantasies, Inc. goodbye. His company's product line was top-notch. Liggett made sure that his products were first-rate, guaranteed customer satisfaction and had the best e-business in the market. In addition to being business-savvy, he had impeccable manners and always sent a thank-you when she critiqued one of his toys. She mentally harrumphed. Ron Capshaw could learn a lot from Liggett.

Meg didn't know what had prompted the thought exactly, but the guy had really rubbed her the wrong way. She'd only done her job, what *Foreplay* had paid her handsomely to do. It wasn't personal. With luck, she'd be able to avoid him for the rest of the show.

"Did Ann ask you about dinner tomorrow night?" Marcus wanted to know as they made their way through the lobby back to the bank of elevators.

Meg nodded. "Yes, she did. Tomorrow night is fine."

"Good," he replied jovially. "I'm looking forward to picking your friend's brain." He paused. "Ann tells me that you have concerns, that perhaps he might embarrass easily." Marcus smiled reassuringly. "Don't sweat it. I'll finesse him."

Great, Meg thought, forcing a wobbly smile. If the penis ring comments were Kent's way of *finessing* they would be in for an excruciatingly long dinner. She hummed noncommittally instead of framing an inane reply.

Furthermore, something in the way he'd lingered over the word finesse in regard to Nick gave her pause.

Marcus wore a mysterious little smile and rocked back on his heels. "He certainly is a fine specimen," he commented lightly. "No wonder your reviews are always so prompt."

"My secret's out," Meg trilled, her unease growing. Marcus's keen interest in Nick's opinion suddenly took on an altogether different meaning. She bit her bottom lip as a particularly disturbing thought surfaced. Meg's eyes widened fractionally as she glanced at Marcus's innocent profile. Nah, Meg thought. No!

Meg said a quick goodbye and exited the elevator on the fifth floor, leaving Marcus to make the climb to his suite solo. She puzzled over his curious behavior and dismissed her suspicions as ludicrous. Chalked her misgivings up to an overactive imagination.

Despite the fact they'd prepped for the dinner, Meg couldn't help but be a little ill-at-ease about tomorrow night. Nick knew the merchandise, but other than the Shiver Cream, he clearly didn't have any interest in ever using the other stuff.

The Shiver Cream.

Her insides quivered with delight at the mere thought of it—of what he'd done with it.

To her.

She relived the sensation of having his finger trail down the side of her neck, the fan of his breath, the feel of his lips as he'd nibbled at her. Her body quivered with renewed desire, her feminine muscles clenched in anticipation.

When he'd planted his big hands on her hips and rocked against her, thrust his tongue in her mouth, she'd simply come apart. Shattered. The sensation hadn't been like anything she'd ever experienced. It had been utterly blissful, without blemish and strangely, she couldn't imagine ever sharing anything so indescribably perfect with another person. Meg slowed as she neared her room, finally letting a truth she'd attempted to bury beneath layers of lust and physical attraction surface.

Nick Devereau was special.

She'd known it from the get-go, had been inevitably drawn to him from the beginning. Something about him compelled her, drew her like a lodestone. Yes, she wanted him, had wanted him from the first moment she'd glimpsed his thrillingly large frame. But it went deeper than that.

Meg had never been prone to sentiment, never longed for a mate the way many of her friends did. She supposed her feelings stemmed from the residual impact of her first so-called love. Meg smiled without humor. The hurt, anger and humiliation. She'd lost her scholarship and had had to work doubly hard to make her career mark. There had never been a great deal of time left for romance, and by the time she realized it, she'd grown too accustomed—too independent—to care that she was the only single person in a party filled with couples. After that hard lesson, having someone to share her life with hadn't been a priority. She'd filled her life with a select few friends, was close to her family and she worked. A lot. She'd learned not to be lonely in her aloneness. Meg's shoulders sagged with an invisible weight.

But she would be lonely now. She knew it. Could feel the beginnings of a void starting to swell deep in her chest.

The sound of Nick's smooth, decadent voice sounded through the door, drawing a reluctant smile.

So he talked to himself? Shouldn't be an endearing habit, but she found the discovery adorable all the same.

Forcing her somber thoughts aside, Meg rapped on the door. She'd left her key card in her purse.

Her purse.

Meg quailed. She'd been gone for at least ten minutes. Plenty of time for him to check out her license, memorize her credit card numbers and scan her check register. Of all the imbecilic things for her to do! A litany of curses streamed through her panic-seized mind.

Thankfully, reason returned before he'd made it to the door. Nick had money of his own—he was an attorney, for pity's sake. Her credit cards and checkbook were safe.

It was her identity that had been jeopardized.

Meg wrestled for composure and managed to summon an overly bright smile by the time he opened the door.

"You're back," he murmured warmly.

That silky baritone made her knees go weak. She peered closely at him, trying to determine if she could read anything in those marvelous heavy-lidded orbs. If he'd practiced any sort of deception while she'd been gone, he certainly hid it well.

God, she hoped he hadn't! She wanted him to be different. To be trustworthy. She was almost sick with dread and worry and, for reasons which escaped her, had attached an unreasonable significance to

whether or not he'd taken the opportunity she'd fool-
ishly given him and gone through her purse.

"Sorry I took so long," Meg apologized. She
stepped around him and made her way deeper into
the room. Everything seemed to be exactly the way
she'd left it, including her purse.

Until she looked more closely. The zipper lay an
inch from closed.

Meg closed her eyes as nausea clawed its way up
her throat. She was so disappointed—a painfully familiar sentiment—that she couldn't even be angry.
Just sick.

Nick—completely oblivious to her bitter regret—
had followed her in and sat down on the end of her
bed. He thumbed through the pay-per-view movie
guide.

"Did you read the journal?" Meg asked, and con-
gratulated herself. She sounded almost normal.

"Yeah, I read it. You're organized."

Meg hummed impatiently. "Yeah. Did you go
through my purse?"

His oh-shit expression, combined with the fact he
didn't readily look up didn't inspire comfort and inclined Meg to assume the worst. She cursed under
her breath. Her knees buckled with defeat, forcing
her to plop down on the bed as well.

"No, I didn't go through your purse," Nick said
soberly.

Meg held up her hand. "Save it, Nick," she
sighed. "The zipper isn't closed."

"I didn't go through your purse," he repeated adamantly. "I almost did. Even picked it up. But I couldn't do it."

"Couldn't?" Interesting term, Meg thought, finally working up the courage to look at him. She admired the fact that he hadn't outright denied everything, that he'd admitted to at least thinking about going through her purse. That took character.

"Couldn't," Nick repeated as his sincere gaze captured hers. He traced a comma on her cheek. "Because if you wanted me to know your real name, you would have told me." He shrugged. "I don't like it—in fact, I hate it—but I'll respect your wishes."

Relief lifted the droop from her shoulders. "Thank you."

"You're welcome." He tipped her chin up for a sweet, lingering kiss. "Now how about that movie?"

"Sure."

Nick ordered the movie, flipped off her bedside light and motioned for Meg to come and lie beside him on her bed. She did, snugly settling her head against his chest. The steady beat of his heart resonated beneath her ear. A sigh of pleasure—of pure contentment—seeped past her lips. It was as though this niche beside him had been carved out especially for her. That this moment—their meeting at this time and at this place—had been predestined. That was a Desiree Moon thought, but Meg savored it all the same.

Since luck had never been her friend, perhaps destiny had decided to intervene on her behalf. A thought struck her.

"I heard you a little while ago," she murmured.

He tensed. "What?"

"A little while ago. Before I came in. I heard you talking to yourself. Is that a habit or an undisclosed psychosis?" She chuckled softly.

She felt him sigh and he nuzzled her more firmly against him. A barb of heat struck her belly. "I have no undisclosed psychoses," he told her, chuckling under his breath. "I was on the phone. Are you going to do this through the whole movie?"

"Do what?"

"Talk."

His shirt rasped her cheek as she smiled. She smoothed her hand over his chest, marveling at the muscle beneath. "Is that your way of telling me to shut up?"

"I wouldn't dream of telling you to shut up. That would piss you off."

Meg laughed. "Well, there are other ways of keeping me quiet."

He stilled. "Yeah?"

"Yeah."

"Like what?"

Meg worked a couple of his buttons loose from their closures, slid her hand across his abdomen. "You still owe me one."

# 10

SHE WAS AT IT AGAIN, Nick thought darkly as he fastened his cuffs. That low hum he'd grown to hate over the past three days buzzed through the wall, straight to his eardrums where the tune raked against his fraught nerve endings and made him want to howl with frustration. Morning, noon and night, he heard it.

On and on and on.

She never moaned like she'd done for him, but Nick's sadistic imagination nonetheless supplied those sweet mewls of pleasure for him. The button he'd been attempting to fasten came off in his hand. Nick swore, shrugged out of the ruined shirt and prowled to his closet for a replacement.

Take last night, for instance. They'd gotten sidetracked as soon as the movie had started because *he owed her one*. A self-satisfied grin curved his lips. He'd paid her back and then some before the night had been over. Nick had never had so much fun being sexually frustrated. They'd kissed, cuddled, stroked and petted until he feared he would expire. Or explode.

Desiree could lead him to the brink of orgasm with

nothing more than the slide of her tongue up his neck. A few bold caresses of those small capable hands. She'd pulled out that Shiver Cream—the most aptly named stuff in the world according to Nick, by God—and they'd emptied it by night's end. It was the most fun Nick had ever had without actually having sex. He led her to orgasm twice—knew it—and yet less than ten minutes after their connecting doors closed Nick had heard it.

The damned vibrator.

He'd been so shocked he'd almost unmanned himself with the toilet seat lid.

And it was worse now, because he couldn't help but wonder which one she was using. The Red Devil? Cupid's Arrow? The Ebony Avenger? Nick's jaw ached. The Stud? With its rotating tip and gyrating balls? He shuddered as a spasm of dread gripped him. The desire to say the hell with his honor was so strong, his need so great, that Nick could barely keep himself in check. He'd had to come up with some pretty ingenious foreplay to prevent them from crossing that invisible line he'd drawn.

He wanted to make love to Desiree more than he wanted his next breath, and yet he couldn't permit that to happen. He'd come here with a hidden agenda, had purposefully fostered a relationship with her in order to discredit her as a critic. Though he knew he couldn't do that now, he was too deep into the ruse and too mesmerized by her to put an end to the charade. Sleeping with her, knowing that he'd been so deceitful, was simply more than he could permit. No matter how desperately he might want to.

No matter how desperately *she* might want him to.

And she wanted him, that was certain. Desiree had had an agenda of her own this week and she'd made Nick a key part of it. Nick couldn't explain how he knew this, he just did.

She wanted him, he wanted her and, because of his initial duplicity, neither one of them were going to be satisfied. No judge could have designed a more hellish punishment, Nick thought ruefully.

Nick bitterly regretted ever picking up her purse. True, he hadn't looked inside though the urge had been almost overwhelming. But the look of betrayal on her face... Nick's gaze turned inward. The disappointment he'd glimpsed in those gorgeous green eyes when she'd thought that he'd broken her trust. She'd crumpled with despair, had been so dejected Nick had felt like the biggest jackass in the world.

At some point in her life, Desiree had been hurt. Badly.

The experience had told him one thing—*he* couldn't hurt her.

She could never know that he'd come here with the purpose of getting her fired. It wouldn't matter that he'd been unable to see the mission through, only that he'd been persuaded to entertain the thought.

As much for his own peace of mind as hers, Nick couldn't permit that to happen. Call him a coward, selfish. Whatever. He swallowed. But he couldn't ever let her find out why he'd sought her out in the first place.

A soft knock sounded at the connecting door, announcing Desiree's unexpected arrival. Was he late? Nick glanced at the bedside clock. No. She was early. Probably nervous, Nick decided as he left the mirror and moved to the door. Probably worried that he wouldn't remember which vibrator had the nuts. He chuckled darkly.

"Hey..." That was all he could manage. The wicked grin he wore froze, then melted away. Several impressions hit him at once. Lots of skin, cleavage, slinky red fabric, sexy heels. He blinked, pulling it all into focus.

Desiree wore her hair down, loose around her bare shoulders, the dark chocolate waves a little fuller than he'd seen it styled so far. Her makeup—which he'd noticed she applied with a light hand—looked the same.

Except for her mouth.

That carnal mouth, which kept Nick in a permanent state of arousal, was painted hooker red. Blood singed his veins as it shot to his groin. His mouth parched. Nick forced his tormented gaze from her lips, inventoried the rest of her delightful body and made an interesting discovery.

She was color coordinated. Mouth, nails, shoes, dress. All hooker red. The dress was short, semitight, strapless and made of some mysterious fabric that looked thin as a butterfly's wing. It managed to reveal a lot of skin, yet left plenty to the imagination.

Nick instantly imagined her out of it.

"Pop quiz," she said. "What's a butt plug?"

Nick recoiled. "What?"

"That's not the look of a merry sex-toy critic," she chided teasingly. Her eyes twinkled. "That horrified there's-a-slug-in-my-soup face will give you away in nothing flat."

Nick huffed a derisive snort, crossed the room and lifted his dinner jacket from the bed. "If he asks me about a butt plug he'll find himself flat on his back and minus a few teeth. No threat, just fact." Nick cast her a grim sideways glance. "If my ass wore a sign, it would read Exit Only."

She cracked up. "A wee bit homophobic, are we?"

"Yes," he said flatly. He shrugged into his jacket. "I like women. Men who like men give me the creeps. I'm not into the whole politically correct scene."

Desiree's smile seemed ominously bright. He frowned. "Have I offended you? Do you have a gay brother or something?"

"No, you haven't offended me—you're entitled to your opinion. And I don't have a brother, I'm an only child." She paused, her expression curiously amused. She strolled to his window, checked out his view of the Atlanta skyline. "I'm just surprised. I would have thought someone as, uh, virile as you would be secure in your own masculinity."

Nick was still lingering on the virile part when the rest of her compliment backhanded him. He grimaced. "I'm perfectly secure in my own masculinity. Didn't you hear me? It's *un*-masculine behavior that bothers me."

He caught her chewing her nail and another warning bell sounded in his head. Something was up, but he didn't know what. "How long is this going to take?" he asked, hoping a subject change would erase some of the angst from her gorgeous profile.

She turned, robbing him of his breath once again. A strange fluttering winged through his chest. "Probably an hour, maybe an hour and a half. Why?" Her brow knitted. "Do you have plans for after dinner?"

Somehow, Nick had gravitated toward her. He pulled her into the circle of his arms, smiled when he felt her relax against him. "I do."

"Do they include me?" she murmured.

"Most definitely. Me, you and a bottle of wine."

"What about a bottle of Shiver Cream?"

He drew back. Lowered his voice to a more intimate level. "I thought we used it all."

"I have more."

Nick arched an appreciative brow. "Good."

"We'd better go," she said, though her heart clearly wasn't in it.

Nick kissed her forehead. "Yeah. Let's get it over with. And don't worry. I'll play my part well. Everything will be fine. What could go wrong?"

WHAT COULD GO WRONG? Meg wondered with dread.

The possibilities were endless.

If her suspicions were correct, one thing in particular could go wrong but Meg refused to entertain the thought. She'd simply have to intervene. Rescue Nick and save Marcus Kent's teeth, she thought, tamping down a hysterical laugh. How the hell had she gotten into this mess? How had things escalated to this comical degree of deception?

Certainly, she enjoyed her job as a critic. She loved the freedom she had to speak her mind, to put into print some of her most scandalous thoughts. Keeping up the pretense of having a lover was pertinent to keeping her job, to ensuring her future success as a top-notch pastry chef. She'd desperately needed Nick to do this for her—she just hadn't counted on her stress level blowing the top off a seismograph.

"Ann called and gave me Marcus's suite number," Meg told him. "He's in twelve-fourteen."

Nick guided her into the elevator and depressed the call button for the twelfth floor. He wore an elegant charcoal suit, Armani or some other top designer, Meg presumed, given the tailored fit and smooth lines, with a crisp white shirt and forest-green silk tie. His tawny locks had been lightly gelled into place, giving him a more polished look. Meg caught a whiff of pricey cologne, a soft woodsy fragrance which suited him perfectly. The scent coupled with his nearness made her knees suddenly weaken with want. Him, her and a bottle of Shiver Cream, indeed.

When this week was up, she'd miss being Desiree Moon. She swallowed tightly, allowed her gaze to once more slide over Nick. More disturbingly, she'd miss him.

"Any last tidbits of advice?" Nick asked, pulling Meg out of the quagmire of emotional quicksand she'd fallen into.

Yeah, Meg thought, remembering her concerns about Marcus. *Stay outta the shower and don't drop the soap.* "Er, just remember everything we've covered," Meg improvised. "I've trained you well, Antonio. Make me proud. They shouldn't suspect a thing."

Admiration clung to his smile. "Damn, you're sneaky."

She fluttered her lashes with exaggerated flirtation. "Don't you mean good?"

"Oh, you're good all right—good at being bad." Nick caught her ridiculously pleased grin. His eyes widened, and he laughed as though unsure of what to make of her. "Is that all it takes to compliment you? Tell you you're good at being bad?"

She pulled a shrug. "Easy, huh?"

Evidently bewildered, he was still peering curiously at her when the elevator slid to a stop on the twelfth floor. He tore his gaze away from her and led her out into the hall. "It's showtime."

Another nervous tremor shook her tummy. Meg pulled in a fortifying breath and walked with Nick down the long carpeted corridor. Marcus's suite was a corner unit located at the end of the hall. Nick rapped a couple of times on the door and within seconds, Marcus's smiling face beamed at them. Particularly at Nick. A shiver of foreboding whispered down her spine.

"Hi!" Marcus said with enthusiasm. "Come on in! Come on in," he boomed with delight.

They went through the introductions again. Marcus played the gracious host, ushered them deep into the suite and, in short order, placed drinks in both their hands. He seemed to linger a fraction overlong when handing Nick his, Meg noted anxiously.

The rooms were spacious, carpeted in a serviceable beige Berber and appointed with cherry-finished reproduction antiques. A large sitting area with a couple of striped camel-backed couches formed an intimate area to chat.

Unease dogged Meg's every step, but Nick appeared to move without difficulty into his role as her lover. He kept her firmly anchored at his side. He continually touched her, held her hand, draped his arm around her shoulder or kept a couple of fingers snugged at the small of her back. But the dizzying contact never ceased. Arousal buzzed along her nerve endings like radio static, a neverending hum of awareness.

After a few more minutes of idle chitchat they moved to the open-spaced living room. Meg and Nick sat hip to hip on one of the comfortable sofas, leaving the other one vacant for Marcus and Ann. Nick casually slung an arm around her shoulders, settled her firmly against him. In her mind's eye, she replanted herself in his lap, removed his shirt and—

"Have you had a good week so far, Desiree?"

While the question had been posed to her, Marcus nonetheless kept his gaze fastened on Nick. Irritation surged, forcing Meg to bite back a brittle smile.

"I have, thanks," Meg replied, injecting an overly bright note into her voice. "Where's Ann?"

"She'll be here shortly."

Good, Meg thought. Perhaps between the two of them they could keep Marcus occupied. So far, Nick seemed to be oblivious to Marcus Kent's keen fascination, but she didn't know how long Nick would continue to think the man was just being extremely polite. For a confessed homophobic, Nick had certainly let Marcus slip beneath the radar. Despite her frazzled nerves, Meg found it perversely funny.

"So, Antonio. What business are you in?" Marcus wanted to know.

"I'm an attorney."

"Oh, is that right? Always thought attorneys got a bad rap." Marcus parked himself on Nick's other side. "You specialize in anything?"

"Corporate law," Nick said smoothly, as though he'd answered the same question hundreds of times. Wearing a bemused smile, Nick scooted over a fraction, allowing more room for Marcus.

"Ah," Marcus said knowingly. "Big business...for a big man." Marcus's gaze raked Nick from head to toe.

Nick's amiable expression faltered.

Time to intervene. "That's right," Meg trilled, her voice pitched higher than usual. Meg wrapped her arms around Nick's waist. "He's *my* big man."

A knock sounded at the door and Marcus excused himself with a smile. "That'll be Ann."

Thank God! Meg thought.

"Desiree?" Nick murmured between his clenched teeth. "What the hell is going on? Is that man doing what I think he's—"

"Please," Meg begged urgently. "We'll leave as soon as dinner is over. I'll owe you one," she promised.

He snorted under his breath. "You're going to owe me more than one."

Both Nick and Meg stood when Ann breezed in. "Sorry I'm late," she apologized. "Apollo's was supposed to have our dinner ready when I got there to pick it up." She smiled ruefully. "But that wasn't the case. Still, I hope you're hungry. We have plenty."

"I'm starved," Nick said. "Are we ready to eat?"

Meg squashed a frown at Nick's overeager ploy, but played along nonetheless. "I'm famished," she lied dramatically.

Truth be told, you couldn't get a kernel of corn down her constricted throat with a slingshot, but she'd have to manage somehow. That portent of doom she carried like an albatross around her neck grew increasingly heavier. A premonition, she feared, of things to come.

"It must take an amazing quantity of food to sustain a man of your considerable size," Marcus remarked with another overt glance at Nick.

Meg felt Nick's fingers twitch in hers.

"Cut it out, Marcus," Ann chided fondly as she transferred carryout boxes from a plastic sack onto the dining table. "You'll embarrass him."

Ann, seemingly familiar with this aspect of her boss's behavior, glanced at Marcus as though he were just a playful puppy, not a sexual predator with his sights set on Meg's man.

"I don't embarrass easily," said Nick. A feral glint stewed in his narrowed gaze. "But I've been told I have a nasty temper."

To Meg's astonishment, Marcus actually shivered. "Oh, do tell."

"Did I mention that I was hungry?" Meg interjected before Nick could react. "In fact, I'm almost light-headed. Is that about ready, Ann? Can I help you with anything?"

"No need to help. It's ready." Ann had doled out the boxes and poured drinks. She gestured for everyone to sit down. "I know this is a little informal, but Marcus can't abide the poor room service of this hotel." She shuddered delicately. "So I took the liberty of ordering Apollo's legendary Chicken Alfredo for us. I hope no one minds."

"It's fine with me," Meg hurried to assure her.

"Me, too," Nick added, sounding relieved at the change in subject.

"In fact, Chicken Alfredo is one of my favorite dishes. I love Alfredo sauce." Meg felt compelled to keep the conversation rolling in any direction but what they'd originally come here to discuss.

The sex toys.

"Speaking of sauce," Marcus said, "what about the new Body Sauce by Risqué Business? Have you had a chance to look at it yet?"

"I have. It's nice. Tastes good and the texture is pleasing. Did Risqué Business send a representative?" Meg asked, hoping to keep the dialogue on the vendors and not the products.

Nick sat beside her, head bowed determinedly over his plate. He kept his mouth full and his fork loaded. The generous portion that had graced his plate had all but vanished.

"Risqué Business did send a representative," Ann remarked. "They've been around for a long time and have always had a good product line."

"What was your take on the Body Sauce?" Marcus asked Nick. Panic clogged Meg's throat. Her gaze darted nervously to Nick.

Nick appeared startled at first, then he looked at her and his gaze darkened with desire. "It tastes all right," he murmured after a beat. "On Desiree. Don't know if I'd like it on ice cream, though."

Marcus and Ann chuckled while a fierce swift heat blanketed Meg from head to toe.

"How did it taste on him?" Marcus asked lightly, but his eyes glittered with something horrifyingly akin to hunger. Flattering Nick would only feed Marcus's voyeuristic appetite, but what choice did she have? Nick had set the rhythm for how this little session would proceed. She wasn't about to hit a discordant note.

She let her gaze slide over his impressive length,

finally coming to stop at his gaze. Licked her lips. "It was delicious. Better than that Raspberry Chocolate Dream we shared the other night."

The innuendo was lost on Marcus, but it didn't keep him from quivering with delight. His eyes practically rolled back in his head. Nick's expression blackened with outrage and every muscle in his body tensed.

With effort, Meg swallowed back an insane burst of laughter. Though things were too ludicrous to take seriously, she didn't think her perverse sense of humor was in Nick's scope of understanding at present. Not when Marcus continued to stare at him with undisguised lust.

Nick had emptied his plate, leaned back in his seat and slung an arm over her shoulder. His fingers swirled a lazy figure eight on her upper arm. Despite the slow, purposeful movement, Meg felt the tension radiating from him. He was ready to snap—Marcus's neck, most likely.

"I'm sure the two of you hear this all the time," Ann said. "But you make an adorable couple. See, Marcus," she went on, gesturing to them with her empty fork. "This is what love looks like. This is why you're in this business."

Meg's tentative smile froze on her face. From the corner of her eye she noticed Nick's drink had stalled halfway between the table and his mouth, and he wore a similar transfixed expression. This is what love looks like?

*Love?*

They liked each other. Lusted, most definitely. But love?

A peculiar tightening squeezed Meg's chest. A fist of bare-knuckled panic slugged her. Her pulse quickened. Tripped. Roared. Nah, she told herself. Not love. Nick was simply doing an excellent job of convincing them that he was her critique partner. He'd only done what she asked him to do and Ann had obviously inferred something altogether different from Nick's admittedly attentive behavior.

That made perfect sense.

Satisfied that she'd rationalized Ann's incorrect assumption into something she could understand, Meg breathed an inaudible sigh of relief. Honestly, love? Like she could handle. Love was out of her comfort zone.

"What about those penis jelly rings I mentioned the other night?" Marcus asked, his tone still light but strangled. He scooted to the edge of his seat. "Do they prolong your erection, Antonio?"

Meg had anticipated this question and quickly formed an answer before Nick could ready his fist for impact with Marcus's face. "We haven't critiqued that particular product, Mr. Kent, and don't intend to. Uh, Antonio, doesn't need any help keeping an erection."

"No, I don't," Nick confirmed adamantly. "And that's all I have to say about that. Desiree, honey—" the endearment held a venomous edge "—if we're going to catch that movie, we'd better go."

Meg supposed he planned to throttle her. She

made an exaggerated show of checking her watch. "Oh, you're right, darling." She quickly stood. "We'd better go."

"B-but what about dessert?" Marcus sputtered. "We've barely touched on any of the other things I wanted to talk about."

"Oh, I think you've touched on enough," Ann remarked, her eyes twinkling with perceptive humor.

"We have dessert waiting in our room," Nick told him, sending Meg a look that smoldered with as much anger as suggestion. He firmly intended on making her pay for his performance—he clearly planned to torture her. Heat funneled low beneath her navel and she mentally shrugged. She was into that.

Nick thanked both of them for the meal and speedily strode to the door.

"Darling, why don't you go and hold the elevator," she suggested sweetly. Without a backward glance, Nick escaped into the hall.

Meg turned to Marcus. Her previous irritation fled as she took in his tragically disappointed frown. After all, she knew exactly how Marcus felt—she, too, had been bowled over by her attraction for Nick. She certainly couldn't fault Marcus's good taste.

"Antonio doesn't like to be finessed," Meg told him. "If I would have suspected this at all, I could have warned you and saved you both some grief." She patted his arm. "Furthermore, he's mine. And he doesn't bat for your team."

Marcus heaved a dramatic sigh. "More's the pity, you lucky girl." He brightened, all business again.

"You are delightful and you're the best reviewer we have. Our Web hits have gone up thirty percent since you came on board. Keep up the good work."

"Thank you." Meg smiled. Her heart lightened at the unexpected praise. "I plan to."

"And now I know why," Marcus countered meaningfully. "Oh, well. Off you go." He tsked under his breath and stared longingly down the hall. "You don't keep a man like that waiting."

Marcus was right. She and Nick had waited long enough...and she owed him one.

Meg would gladly give it to him, too—if he didn't kill her first.

# 11

NICK HAD ALREADY BOARDED the elevator and was patiently holding the door for her when Meg finally caught up with him. She flinched at his thunderous expression. Clearly he hadn't found the episode as amusing as she had. Rather than lean against him as she had the entire night, she lounged against the wall and stared innocently at the ceiling.

"Well," she said when he didn't immediately say anything. She took a page from Lucy Ricardo's book, huffed an exaggerated breath and exclaimed, "Boy am I glad that's over."

His eyes bugged. "*You're* glad it's over?"

Meg winced. That crap might have worked with dear ol' Ricky, but Nick wasn't about to let it fly. "S-sure. Aren't you?"

"Immensely," he growled.

Silence stretched between them once again. Meg peeked at him from the corner of her eye. He stood still as stone, jaw clenched tight and lips compressed in a thin hard line. He didn't look like a man who wanted to talk, but Meg felt compelled to cast another line into the old conversational pond. "I enjoyed my chicken," she remarked inanely.

"I might have," he returned tightly. "If I hadn't had to inhale it."

Obviously Nick didn't share Meg's desire to pretend nothing had happened, and she supposed she couldn't blame him. She'd likely be unnerved if she'd spent the evening fending off advances from Ann. Meg fidgeted uncomfortably. Heaved an internal sigh. "I'm sorry."

Nick finally looked at her, smiled without humor. "For what? My being the butt of your joke? Or offering me as a sexual sacrifice to your editor?" He snorted. Passed a hand wearily over his face. "If I didn't like you so much, I'd probably throttle you."

Ordinarily Meg would have lingered in the delight his liking her brought, but right now her outrage prevented her from enjoying the moment. She blinked, astounded. "Offering you as a sexual sacrifice? Is that what you think just happened?"

"Well, isn't it?"

"No!"

Nick's brow creased skeptically. "You mean to tell me that you didn't know he was gay?"

"I, uh—" Meg faltered, unable to finish.

His lips curled into a mockery of a smile. "I thought so. I knew you needed me to go and help you, but I never expected to double as the entertainment."

"I didn't know he was gay," Meg relented, feeling guilty for not sharing her suspicions. She'd prepared him for everything else—she should have prepared him for this as well. "I suspected," she clarified. "But I didn't know. Furthermore, you didn't double as the entertainment. The whole situation was just so completely ludicrous, I couldn't help but get tickled."

Nick's snort of derision wasn't encouraging.

"I mean, I'd unwittingly asked a homophobic man to pose as my critique partner and graphically discuss sex toys with a gay man who happened to be my boss and who happened to be lusting after you, too." She sucked in a breath. Chewed her lip. "How was I to know that Marcus Kent would be more interested in you than he would be in the male hetero opinion I'd been told he wanted? And by the time I suspected anything...it was too late. He'd already started hungrily stalking you around the suite."

Nick seemed to mull that over. He shuffled his feet, cleared his throat. "A gay man asked me about my erection. Hit on me. Do you know how disturbing that is?"

"I imagine it's very disturbing," Meg conceded, virtually wilting with relief. His voice no longer sounded clipped and wounded. Just mildly outraged. Funny that she should find that adorable. "But if I were you, I'd be flattered."

Eyes wide, he swiveled to look at her. "Flattered?"

"Yes. Of course."

"Flattered." He expelled a disbelieving breath. "Go with it," he told her, planting a hand on his hip. "I want to hear what sort of spin you're going to put on this to make it sound better."

Meg shrugged, sidled closer to him. "It's simple. You're irresistible to both sexes. Of all the men traipsing through this hotel, Marcus set his discriminating sights on you."

"And that's supposed to make me feel better? That he thought I swung his way, too?"

Meg giggled. She couldn't help it. "No, that he found you so attractive, he pursued you even though he thought you were straight." She tiptoed and gently kissed his cheek. "And taken," she murmured. Tiptoed and kissed his jaw. "And unbelievably irresistible." Tiptoed and kissed the corner of his lips. "And I know exactly how he feels, because I haven't been able to resist you from the start. I have a confession to make," Meg told him. She lowered her voice. "I'm in lust with you."

His stony facade had begun to crack after the first kiss and crumbled away altogether with that last sentence. With a groan of defeat, Nick clamped his mouth hungrily over hers. Giddy with relief, Meg shuddered as his tongue swept past her teeth, plundered wildly. God, she loved the way he kissed. Hard, then soft, a sweep of his tongue, a dizzying suckle. She parlayed his every advance, countered each erotic move of his sinfully talented tongue with one of her own.

She'd been waiting for this all night. Forever.

Breathing heavily, Nick collapsed against the elevator wall and urgently molded her to him. His powerful arms banded around her, forcing a moan of delight between their joined mouths. A volcano of heat erupted in Meg's belly, flowed determinedly to her womb. Her feminine folds slickened, her breasts plumped with want, grew heavy.

In the dim recesses of her mind, Meg heard the soft tinkling of a bell. Almost like an internal timer, heralding the end of her time spent in a lonely bed.

"We haf'a ge'roff th' el'vator," Nick murmured between their linked lips.

Meg slid her hands beneath his dinner jacket, felt the muscles at the small of his back bunch with pleasure. "Wha'—?"

Nick tore his mouth from hers, removed her hands from under his jacket. Breathing hard, he smiled crookedly. "We have to get off the elevator," he repeated, his voice rough with desire. His eyes were dark and slumberous, so compelling Meg longed to launch herself back at his mouth.

But he was right. They didn't need to do it in the elevator.

Yet.

Nick threaded his fingers through hers, tugged her down the hall. In short order, he'd unlocked the door and guided her inside. They instantly groped for each other again. The door hadn't even closed behind them before Nick backed her up against the wall in the foyer. His lips once again found hers, descended with unerring accuracy. He fed greedily at her mouth, lifted her up and anchored her around his hips. Those strong fingers kneaded her exposed thighs. Longing barbed through her, forced a cry of delight from her throat. A dull throb commenced between her thighs.

Nick had left her mouth and began a thorough expedition down the side of her neck. "God, you taste good," he murmured thickly.

Meg clawed his coat from his shoulders, knocked it to the floor. She loosened his tie and urgently tugged his shirt from his waistband. Her palms itched to touch his skin, to feel those powerful muscles moving beneath her hands.

Moving inside her.

She'd never wanted anything more in her life than this moment with him. Meg frantically worked at the buttons on his shirt, cursed when she couldn't release them from their closures.

Nick chuckled at her impatience. Stilled her hands at his chest. "Hey, let's slow this down a bit."

Meg bit back a wail of frustration. She'd waited too long for this to slow down now! "Let's don't and say we did." Chest heaving like a bellows, she struggled with his shirt again. "Get naked."

He blinked, then burst out laughing. "You first."

Something came over Meg. Confidence sprang from some hidden internal well. Just like that night in the restaurant. She drew back, tossed him a wicked smile, and with an exaggerated swing of her hips started toward the bed. She turned to face him, watched him swallow as she reached behind her. The movement thrust her breasts against the sexy material and, given his swift intake of breath, he hadn't failed to notice it.

Her zipper whined as she quickly drew it down her back. Meg released the dress and the cool gauzy fabric whispered down her skin and puddled around her feet. She hadn't worn a bra—only a thong. His heated gaze singed her.

"Do you need any help with your shirt?" Meg asked, when he didn't readily move. Hell, she hadn't given him a you-can-look-but-don't-touch order. She was ready...willing...

His breath left him in a whoosh and he blinked as though coming out of a trance. He gave a curiously resigned sigh, as though he'd come to some sort of weighty decision, then he grasped the edges of his shirt and ripped it off. Buttons flew, ricocheted off the walls. "No."

Meg jumped, squealed with delight. "I guess not. Was that expensive?"

He shucked his pants and briefs. "Who cares?"

Meg barely had time to appreciate his incredible form again before he propelled himself toward her. They fell onto the bed amid laughter and giggles.

"Now where were we?" Nick mused with a husky rumble, coming to rest alongside her. She felt small and protected. Cocooned.

Hot.

Meg's lids fluttered closed. The decadent feel of his skin against hers was heavenly. Her breath shuddered out of her at the wholly intimate contact. Nick gently trailed a finger down the middle of her chest, stopped mere inches below her belly button. Then retraced the sensitive path. He swirled a leisurely figure eight around her puckered breasts. A shiver shook her from the inside out, leaving a warm tingle in its wake.

"Right about here, I'd say," Meg replied. She cupped his jaw, slid her fingers into the hair at his temples and offered her lips up for another kiss. This one started out slow, with lazy, probing strokes of his tongue, long deep sucks at her mouth. Promises of things to come.

But not quickly enough. Meg upped the tempo, ran her hands along the intriguingly ridged muscles of his abdomen. Lightly scored his skin with her nails and was gratified when his agonized hiss reached her ears.

Her feminine muscles clenched, dewed more with anticipation, readying for him. She felt his hardened length nudge her hip and a frantic yearning cried from her womb.

He wanted her, she knew it, and yet instead of surrendering control of the situation and letting pleasure lead them where it would, Nick still annoyingly attempted to maintain control.

All this kissing was good, but she'd really like to move it along. She wanted it...her way...the way she'd dreamed it would be.

The dirty talk had worked before.

Meg drew back. "I want you to kiss me—" she circled her nipple with an index finger "—here."

His lids dropped to half-mast and his breath stuttered from his lungs. Then he smiled. It was one of those, Baby-you-don't-know-what-you've-gotten-yourself-into smiles that held more male satisfaction, confidence and promise than humor, and absolutely thrilled Meg to her little toes.

She had him.

"Like this, I wonder," he whispered. He leaned down and barely touched her nipple with the tip of his tongue.

Meg gasped as little hot curls of pleasure looped through her.

"Or like this?" He wrapped his lips around the sensitive peak and gently suckled.

The curls of pleasure spun more tightly, tugged a reciprocating thread mysteriously attached to her sex. Her breath lodged in her throat.

"Or like this, maybe?" This time he sucked hard, flattening the crown of her breast to the roof of his mouth.

Meg's body bowed off the sheet. Stars burst behind her lids as the pleasure burst into white-hot flames.

He chuckled softly, knowingly, his warm breath breezing over her wet peak. "I thought so."

Then he did it again. And again. He squeezed her, licked her, fed at her until she thought she would quiver into nothingness. Dissolve into a puddle of pure want.

Meg longed to explore him in turn, and quickly morphed that longing into action. If her nipples were this sensitive, it stood to reason his would be, too.

She found one of the ruddy tips beneath his tawny masculine hair and gently plucked. He trembled and a low guttural moan rumbled from his throat.

Gratified, Meg's lips curled into a feline grin and she repeated the process. Ran her hands over the smooth yet delineated planes of his back. Her palms feasted on him, marveled at the latent power concealed behind supple sinew and solid masculine bone structure.

To her immense delight, he'd begun a similar investigation. He palmed her breasts once more, weighed them carefully, slid a hand down the front of her belly, over her hip and dallied around her inner thigh. Renewed need kindled and burst into ravenous flame. Meg involuntarily arched, silently begging him to stroke the part of her which most longed for his attention.

He didn't.

She whimpered.

Instead, and to her further frustration, his fingers dipped to the sensitive skin behind her knee. Undoubtedly, he'd be at her ankles next. Meg resisted the impulse to wail.

Maybe she just needed to show him. Meg shifted onto her side and rested one knee against his naked hip, opening herself up to him. Then she reached down and tentatively took him in her hand. Nick sucked in a harsh breath at the contact, and she felt him throb against her palm.

Several impressions hit her at once—hot, hard, smooth and large.

She'd never held a real live penis before—hell, she'd barely felt one the first time let alone held it— and this was a singularly intoxicating sensation.

She'd known what to expect, of course, but clinical experience hadn't prepared her for the genuine article. She'd expected him to be hard, she'd known he'd be large.

But the heat emanating from him surprised her, as did the incredibly soft skin encasing the rigid length of his arousal. Meg curiously skimmed the sides, glided her hand over the super-smooth tip. She took him fully in her hand once more, gently tugged the hot slippery skin back and forth along the length of him. Nick hissed, uttered a soft oath. Emboldened, she cuddled his testicles, reveled in the silkiness. He groaned savagely.

Meg was so caught up in her exploration of him, the first brush of his fingers against her feminine curls ripped the breath from her lungs.

Nick gently pushed her onto her back and once again fastened his greedy mouth at her breast. His fingers traced, then parted her nether lips. "Mmmm, so wet," he muttered thickly.

He grazed the sensitive bud hidden there, sending a bolt of glorious sensation through her alternately tense and languid body. Yeah, that. That was the spot. Oh, right there. That's what she needed. Craved. Now if he would just—

"Like that, do you?" Nick breathed against her. She could hear his grin, damn him.

"Y-yes," she managed, desperately squirming against his finger. "Do. It. Again."

Nick stroked her, purposely avoiding the one spot

she most wanted massaged. "Hmmm…what's the magic word?"

"Now!"

Nick chuckled softly. Then simultaneously sucked hard at her nipple and slipped one long finger deep into her channel. Meg's eyes widened, then shut as a torrent of pleasure rippled through her veins and concentrated at the apex of her thighs. Oh, hell. This was— She could— She squirmed shamelessly against him. Whimpered with need. He methodically worked his finger in and out of her, massaged her secret nub with his knuckle. Played at her breast.

It felt wonderful and yet somehow it wasn't enough. She was starving still, hungry for more. It was as though he'd given her a crust of bread and she wanted the whole loaf.

She wanted him inside her. Needed him inside her. Now.

"Please, Nick," she whimpered, not ashamed to beg.

"Please, what?"

The bastard, Meg mentally railed. He knew what. She'd known he would torture her, had known he would pay her back for tonight. He might have absolved her of guilt where Kent was concerned, but he apparently had something to prove to himself— some crackbrained male thing she'd likely discover later. But later wasn't soon enough.

"P-please," she tried again. "Oh, please."

Nick knuckled her harder, crooked one finger deep

inside until he brushed a hidden patch of super-sensitive flesh. "You want this?" he asked huskily.

A sound, part cry, part moan broke free of her throat as he once again catapulted her to near release. A screw of heat tightened below her navel, built steadily, but didn't deliver her to climax.

Meg shook her head, unable to form the words.

"Tell me what you want."

He wanted her to say it. Fine. Whatever. She didn't care. He'd maintained control—she'd lost it, and was beyond caring. Game, set, match. "I want *you*. All the way inside *me*."

Nick dragged his finger through her folds, kissed her deeply. He magically produced a condom, rolled it swiftly down his hardened length. His caramel gaze fastened on hers, that invitation to sin blatantly present in those gorgeous heavy-lidded orbs. "All you had to do was say the words."

Amen!

She welcomed his weight as he positioned himself between her thighs, nudged between her drenched folds and swiftly pushed fully, completely inside her.

A silent scream of pleasure rose from Meg's throat. Her world went black, then lights danced behind her lids. She arched off the sheet, stunned at the intimate yet foreign invasion.

"Man, you're tight." Nick tensed inside her, held perfectly still. His gaze met hers, and a curious shadow passed over his face. "Am I— Am I hurting you?"

Meg tentatively rocked against him, lifted her hips

to draw him more deeply inside her. Her muscles involuntarily clenched, detonating another firework display of bright sensation. "No," she breathed.

"Are you cert—"

"I'm positive," she insisted, her words tormented, her body tortured. Dammit, she'd finally gotten him where she wanted him and he still held back! She was determined to make him lose it. Make him beg, too.

Meg lifted her hips, tilted them more firmly into his. She instinctively flexed her feminine muscles, drawing him more deeply inside her. "Do you have any idea how wonderful this feels?" she asked him. She leaned forward and nipped at his lips. She wanted to scream, wanted to burst into a chorus of *Hallelujah!*

"Oh, I think I have a pretty good idea," came his strangled, but clearly amused reply.

His arms braced beside her, Meg watched as his face reflected a smidgen of her own torture. His brow furrowed and a sheen of sweat coated his magnificent body as he fought to maintain control. She could feel him there, pulsing inside her. She flexed around him again, and again. Smoothed her hands down his back, grasped the twin muscles of his rear and pulled him closer against her.

He finally snapped.

"Bloody hell," he roared. Then to Meg's almost unbearable delight thrust powerfully into her.

She met him halfway the second time, and the next and the next as he slammed into her. Deep hard thrusts that thrilled her to her very soul. A constant game of withdraw and retreat that steadily built and built, like a circle slowly turning on itself until its shape was indistinguishable.

He kissed her neck, suckled her nipples, seemingly unable to taste enough of her. Meg reciprocated in kind, fascinated with his incredibly broad shoulders. She kissed them, nipped at them. Frantically met him thrust after thrust. She anchored her legs around his waist, bowed and arched, begged—anything to get him more deeply inside her. He filled her to the point of pain, but it was a perfect blend of exquisite pleasure and delicious pain.

He plunged again and again. Deeper, harder, faster and faster until he finally led her to the edge and sent her flying over the precipice. For one fleeting instant, Meg's body forgot to breathe. Everything inside her stilled in awe of the cataclysmic eruption of magnificent release.

Nick shuddered violently atop her, another thick hot rush of sensation. Breathing hard, he collapsed against her, but quickly rolled them to where the bulk of his weight landed on the mattress. He snuggled her against him.

Meg's own breath came in erratic little puffs. She blinked, still basking in the glow of her first real orgasm with a man inside her. It had been a full body experience, from the very hair on her scalp down to the tips of her toes. Included every single cell that made up her body. Utterly incredible. Indescribably hedonistic. Whoever had coined the phrase ''better than sex'' had obviously never had the kind of orgasm Nick had just given her.

In fact, Meg thought with a small smile, she liked it so much she wanted another one. She wanted as many as she could get before her week as Desiree was up.

# *12*

---

RON HAD BEEN RIGHT. Though it didn't matter because he'd never use the information against her as planned, Ron had been right. And, to add insult to injury, he'd forsaken his honor in order to slake his lust.

She might as well have been a virgin for all the experience he now knew she had.

Dread settled like a dead weight in the pit of Nick's gut, preventing him from enjoying the aftermath of the bar-none, hands down, unequivocal best sex of his life.

The realization had slammed into him the second he'd thrust inside her. She'd been so tight, so snug around him that it had taken a moment of quiet reflection to realize that she hadn't been a virgin...not completely anyway. But close enough for Nick to wish he hadn't thrust into her like a battering ram.

But he hadn't been able to hold back any longer, had forced her to beg him. Punishment for making him feel out of control, inside out and all the other conflicting emotions she'd stirred in sentimental territory best left uncharted.

He'd plunged into her, confident despite niggling doubts to the contrary, that she was a seasoned lover.

God knows she'd played the part of a veteran between the sheets. She'd gotten him off with her toes, had talked dirty to him, for pity's sake. Shocked him. She'd been a walking contradiction, a femme fatale one minute, the vulnerable innocent the next. Still, he'd had doubts, and if he hadn't been so blinded by lust, so gratified by her eagerness to be with him, he might have heeded those mental warnings more closely.

His cheeks puffed as he exhaled mightily. He really should have known, Nick berated himself now. She'd dropped little clues along the way. Nick mentally ticked them off. Not bringing a lover with her to the trade show. No record of said lover in her journal. And that little comment she'd made in his lap about it being better than she ever dreamed.

The evidence had been before him the entire time, but he'd been so blinded by lust, he hadn't been able to see past his pecker. So determined for her to be the opposite of what Ron thought that he'd deluded himself into thinking she was everything she claimed to be.

Other than Desiree Moon, though, what exactly had she ever claimed to be? To him, anyway? Just herself, Nick knew. Just a pastry chef/sex-toy critic.

True, she might be misrepresenting herself to her boss, to the owners and patrons of the adult-toy industry—but she'd never misrepresented herself to him. Not once.

And so what if she'd said Ron's products sucked? They did. Would Ron's products have sucked if she'd had a real critique partner helping her review them? Nick snorted, recalling the horrible-tasting panties and icky lubricating gel. Most definitely.

And wouldn't Ron's company go bust anyway? It would if the rest of his products were as bad as the ones Desiree had shown Nick.

Fact of the matter was, she wasn't hurting anyone, least of all his brother. As he'd predicted, Ron had made her his scapegoat. Desiree shouldn't have to pay for Ron's crappy product line with her side job. Nick had seen her journal, knew how she prided herself on organization, attention to detail. She might be fabricating a little here, fudging a little there, but she did a good job. Nick couldn't deny that.

He swore silently. There had to be some way out of this. Had to be some way to make everything right. To make everyone happy. To assuage the perpetual guilt he felt for having the privilege of his father's love. To keep his mother's retirement safe. To help Ron without giving him another handout. Nick tunneled his fingers through his hair. He just needed a little bit more time to—

A telltale buzz commenced from the bathroom where Desiree had gone to freshen up, fracturing Nick's turbulent thoughts.

He lay there, slack-jawed, stunned beyond reason. His mind blanked, then raced. His head jerked in the direction from the bathroom, landed on the meager slice of light pushing through the partially open door.

She'd just left the damned bed! Just a few minutes ago, the force of her orgasm had milked him dry. How could she possibly require…servicing so soon? How could she leave his bed and take up one of those damned impersonal toys?

Insulted, annoyed, outraged and a couple of other disturbing sentiments he didn't care to name jolted through him. His jaw ached from clenching it so hard.

Nick lay there, tried to will the sound away—the image away—and failed miserably. Dammit, he'd suffered enough indignity tonight at her expense— that leering jackass she called her boss surfaced in his mind. He shouldn't have to suffer this as well. He shouldn't have to listen to her masturbate within moments of leaving his bed.

It was outside of enough.

He had the equipment she needed, and, if he hadn't done it to her satisfaction—though after that off-the-sheets orgasm, he couldn't imagine that he'd failed—he'd gladly give her a repeat performance until he purged her seemingly perpetual need for release from her gorgeous little body. All she had to do was tell him. She'd certainly been vocal about what she wanted up until this point. Nick refused to let some plastic dong with batteries outdo him in bed. It simply wasn't acceptable.

Dragging the sheet with him, Nick bounded from the bed, stalked to the bathroom and, after a moment's hesitation, gently nudged the door open. His gentle nudge sent the door banging against the wall.

She jumped and her surprised reflection stared at him from the mirror.

She smiled around her toothbrush, surreptitiously spit and rinsed her mouth.

Her electric toothbrush.

Nick blinked repeatedly. Relief jimmied a strangled laugh from his throat. He rubbed a hand over his suddenly flushed neck. All those times he'd heard that low buzzing hum, she'd been brushing her teeth—not playing the leading role in a masturbation musical like he'd assumed. He'd tortured himself needlessly. Took matters into his own hands to the tune of her electric toothbrush—needlessly. Humiliation burned his cheeks.

"Sorry," she said, giving him a perplexed look. "Was I taking too long?"

"Uh, no. Just wanted to make sure you were all right." Of course, he could have called out from the bedroom instead of bursting into her bathroom like a zealous rookie on his first drug bust. Geez. He was pathetic. He'd been a complete and total wreck since he started this damned farce. He hadn't been himself at all.

She shrugged self-consciously, gestured with her toothbrush. "My dad's a dentist. I have to practice good oral hygiene. It's a rule."

"Oh." Inane, he knew, but the best he could do at present. She still looked delightfully rumpled. Her hair tumbled around her shoulders in wild disarray and a becoming rose bloomed on her cheeks. She'd slipped on a short, light-blue robe with daisies scattered all over it. The sash had been tied loosely, leaving a deep vee open down the front. Her breasts played hide-and-seek beneath the slinky fabric, giving him a glimpse of creamy swells and pale pink nipples. The hem of her robe hit her at midthigh, revealing legs that were tanned, toned and nicely shaped. Nick caught a metallic flash at her feet, and noticed a sterling silver toe ring on her left foot.

Just like that, he went hard.

"I was thinking about taking a shower," she told him, forcing his gaze from her sexy toe. Her lips curved knowingly. "Wanna join me?"

It was as though she'd stepped from his fantasies. She might as well have said, "You're the best lover I've ever had, you have the biggest rod I've ever seen and my sole desire in life is to blow you. Here's your beer, and the remote." At least, that's what Little Nick heard.

She shrugged out of the robe, let it pool around her feet. She bent low, turned on the tap and adjusted the spray.

Damn, her ass was perfect. Nick swallowed tightly. He didn't want to appear too easy. "Depends," he said, as though he really had a choice. As though he wouldn't mind skipping the shower altogether and taking her on the vanity.

She smiled, recognizing the ploy. "On what?"

"On whether or not I get to wash your back."

She slipped behind the shower curtain, and he watched her silhouette through the thin transparent hanging. "Sure. You can wash my back, so long as

I can wash your front.'' She arched languorously. ''With my mouth.''

To hell with being easy, Nick thought. He wanted her.

MEG LOWERED THE VOLUME on the television so as not to wake Nick and settled more peacefully beside him. The room was pitch-black, save for the dancing shadows and bluish light emanating from the TV. An empty pizza box and soda cans littered the small table in the corner of the room and the faint scent of pepperoni, shampoo and sex mingled in the air.

It had always been her understanding that men generally didn't care to linger in a woman's bed after sex, so she'd been pleased when Nick had commandeered an extra pillow from his room, then stretched himself out on her side of the bed. They'd talked for a while, then he'd drifted off to sleep.

Meg gazed at him now and an unfamiliar longing rose in her breast. A tremulous smile drifted around her lips and she resisted the urge to brush his tousled hair back from his forehead. To skim the pad of her thumb over his lips.

Nick had rolled over on his side, twisting the sheet around his magnificent body. One arm rested beneath his pillow and the other along his thigh. His face, so relaxed in sleep, was still the same combination of planes and angles, yet different somehow. Not boyish—there was nothing boyish about the way this man looked—but still…different. Not relaxed, Meg decided. Everyone relaxed when they slept. Nick seemed…less guarded.

He'd been particularly on guard after their shower. His phone had rung a couple of times, but he hadn't answered it. When she'd looked at him questioningly, he'd shrugged and said they'd leave a message.

Nick had told her that he'd want her name at the end of this week, but he hadn't asked for it. At least, not yet. And if he did, what would she say? Would she give it to him? Or would she keep to her one-week-as-Desiree rule and simply chalk this up as the best sexual experience of her life and leave it at that? Preserve this memory unblemished. When she'd made the decision to be Desiree Moon for the week, to leave her inhibitions behind, she'd never considered that she'd be leaving Nick behind when the week was over. She did now, and the thought saddened her more than she cared to admit. Her feelings tumbled and jumbled, banged around her heart like a pinball.

Meg had just never counted on liking him. Genuinely liking him. She'd been attracted to him, wanted him desperately. But she hadn't initially considered anything beyond the physical. But then, he'd gone and made her laugh, made her crave his company, made her long to be with him.

That's why women were less eager to engage in no-strings-attached affairs, Meg realized. Most of them couldn't leave it at great sex, and regrettably she appeared to be one of them. There were always emotional loose ends left to be tied up.

More time spent with him would undoubtedly lead to additional heartache when their relationship ended, but it was a sacrifice Meg planned to make. She planned to spend every second she could with him—in and out of bed—until Friday. Regrettably, this would be her only no-strings stint and she had every intention of milking it for all it was worth.

Meg's thoughts bounced around, settling on a more pleasant topic.

She'd had her first *good* sexual encounter with a man.

The last and only time she'd been tipsy and slightly horny. He'd been attractive and, fool that she was, she'd fancied herself in love. Bad motivation, worse circumstances.

She'd squandered her virginity with a premature ejaculator who had possessed all the finesse of a drunken goat. A big-mouthed, drunken goat who'd bragged about the unmemorable encounter and ultimately cost her the scholarship she'd counted on to finish her education. It was a mistake that still haunted her, that she still regretted. She'd just never repeated the mistake. That experience had taught her to be selective to the point of paranoia.

But it had paid off.

She'd gotten Nick.

The years of celibacy had been worth it, since they'd led her to him. Meg still marveled at their joining. The feel of him, the whole hardened length of him, had been the most indescribably perfect sensation she could ever hope to have.

She'd felt full, a connection in excess of the physical.

Every particle in her being sang with the junction of their bodies. It was as though his presence had tripped the last tumbler of a lock into place, as though everything she'd done or ever hoped to do had been tied into that moment.

Nick had stilled above her when they first came together and an unreadable expression had crossed his face. He'd stared wonderingly at her for interminable moments and Meg suspected she hadn't been the only one who'd experienced the magic of that moment. Delight settled over her like a comfortable blanket. Clearly Nick had felt it, too.

Meg smiled when she considered that she hadn't allowed either one of them to linger in that special moment for long—she'd been too impatient, too ready for him to pause for sentimentality.

She still couldn't believe how forward she'd been, how she'd spoken to him. She wished she could conjure a blush—felt like she should—but the self-consciousness required to pull it off simply wasn't there. Quite frankly, she liked to shock him, liked the way his eyes widened, darkened, and finally capitulated when she said those naughty things to him. It gave her a rush, and obviously him, too, or he wouldn't respond to her shocking behavior as he did.

Another smile rolled around Meg's lips. Nick was a bad boy waiting to happen—he just didn't know it yet. He still had that control issue she needed to take care of.

Meg understood. She had control issues as well. Case in point, the handcuffs. The necessary trust to put that much faith in another person was something that Meg didn't know if she'd ever possess. But for the first time she realized that she might be able to get to that place, to surrender that control.

Still, her hang-ups aside, she still didn't like for Nick's issues to apply to her and how they made love. He'd seemed to set personal parameters around everything in his life, and he needed to learn that some things weren't meant to be cordoned off and compartmentalized. Some things required a go-with-the-flow attitude and everything that was questionable didn't necessarily translate to "bad."

For instance, the adult toys. She could tell from the outraged, slightly arrogant look on his face that he didn't care for them. Granted, there were some that were definitely out of the realm of her understanding. But not all of them. She'd shown him that with the Shiver Cream, but Meg thought he'd probably require several more lessons to completely eradicate that narrow-minded mentality.

Her gaze landed on him once more. Longing kindled again. She'd gladly accept the challenge.

Nick opened his eyes, startling her. "I dozed off," he said, his voice rough with sleep.

She grinned. Gave in to the urge and trailed her fingers across his cheek. "You did."

"Sorry," he mumbled.

"Don't be." She yawned. "I'm tired, too."

Nick snaked an arm around her middle and snuggled her up against him. Contentment swelled inside her, resulting in a small satisfied sigh. "What are your plans for tomorrow?" he asked.

"I'm supposed to do another question-and-answer session in the afternoon."

He nuzzled her neck. "Blow it off."

She laughed. "Why?"

"Because I want to be with you. Let's go somewhere. Do something. What do you say?"

Oh, it was tempting. They could spend the day together, just like a real couple. She'd already tentatively formed special plans for tomorrow night. She wanted to make their last day and night together as memorable as it could possibly be. By noon Friday, this would all be over. Her stint as the uninhibited Desiree Moon would be finished.

"Come on," he prodded at her prolonged hesitation. "I'll take you wherever you want to go."

Good, Meg thought. Take me home with you. She mentally gasped at the thought. Dammit, she couldn't start thinking this way—in terms of forever—it would ruin everything. She cleared her throat. "Don't you have anything you're supposed to do? Is your business in town finished?"

He hesitated only a beat, but she felt it. "No, I'm done," he said. "Tomorrow's mine. Share it with me," he urged huskily.

"Okay. I'll call Ann in the morning and tell her that I can't do that other session." Satisfied with her decision, she relaxed further against him. "It hadn't been planned in the beginning, anyway, so it shouldn't be a problem. Ron Capshaw requested I do another one," she said drolly. "I can't imagine why, though. Remember? He's the one who heckled me during the first one."

The smooth rise and fall of Nick's chest against her back momentarily stilled. "Yeah. I remember."

His voice sounded strained, angry almost, making Meg smile. Apparently the idea of Ron Capshaw bothering her disturbed him. Meg had never had a man—besides her father—so blatantly concerned for her happiness, her well-being. She could handle the Rons of the world, but she liked knowing that someone had her back if she couldn't. She could get used to having a protector, Meg thought, her chest lightening with joy. "Oh, well. I doubt he'll be heartbroken if I don't show up. So, where are you going to take me?" she asked.

"Well, I'm going to take you in the elevator, in the coat closet, in a phone booth, in a cab, in—"

Meg laughed out loud at his outrageous litany. "That all sounds promising, but I want to know where you are taking me *tomorrow*."

Exaggerated confusion creased his brow. He scratched his temple. "I'm sorry. Isn't that what I just answered?"

"Keep it up and you'll be lucky to take me back to bed," she teased.

"Guess again, baby. I have you in bed right now."

Meg growled in warning.

Laughing, Nick surrendered. He kissed her neck, banded her more closely to him, inadvertently setting off another blast of desire. "Where do you want to go?"

Meg grinned, purposely arched her rump against his semi-hard erection. "Dunno about tomorrow. But right now I'd like a trip to the moon."

She felt him harden completely. Nick growled, rolled her round to face him. Planted a long, slow kiss on her lips. "One trip to the moon coming up."

He took her to the moon and back again, buzzed by a few stars and gave her a tour of the entire galaxy before finally settling back down to earth.

Nick was one hell of a pilot.

# *13*

---

"I SAID I'M WORKING on a solution and I am," Nick repeated patiently. "You've just got to give me some more time and let me do things my way."

Nick glanced through his connecting door, made sure that Desiree was still in the shower. Despite virtually no sleep, neither one of them had been inclined to linger in bed this morning. They'd both wanted to get the most of the day.

"What are you talking about, your way?" Ron fired back. "Since when did my plan involve doing things your way?"

Nick struggled to keep his voice neutral, to quell the instant surge of anger his brother's typical braggart response incited. Only the knowledge that Ron was truly desperate to see this business succeed kept Nick from blistering his ears with a few select oaths. "Since you asked me to help you, remember?" Nick reminded him tightly.

Ron laughed without humor. "We both know that if I'd simply asked you to help me, you would have said no. I had to browbeat you into doing it. It's no wonder you don't have any respect for me, any faith. You've kept a running list of every failure and have never—never—shown the least little bit of faith in me." Ron sighed. "Just like Dad."

That comment was uncomfortably true, Nick realized with a start. He filed it away for future consideration.

"Are you going to help me or not, Nick?" Ron asked after a beat of tense silence. "Is she a fraud or not? I need to know."

Nick neatly dodged the question. "You asked to have her do another Q&A session," Nick said. "For what reason?"

"How else am I supposed to discredit her? Send everyone a postcard telling them that she's a fraud?" He snorted. "I need to put an end to her reviews at this show."

"That won't be necessary, I can guarantee that. Besides, she's not doing the session because she's going to be with me."

"With you?" Ron swore. "You weren't supposed to start dating her, you were just supposed to get close enough to her to see if she was on the up and up, to see if she was a fraud. What's going on, Nick?" Ron asked suspiciously.

"Nothing. You just need to let me do things my way. Back off and I'll take care of everything."

"Whatever," he finally huffed. "It's getting down to the wire here. We're running out of time."

Didn't he know it? Nick thought, absently rubbing the bridge of his nose. "I'll handle it," Nick repeated.

Ron sighed gratefully into the phone. "Okay. I

know you will. It's just, I'm going crazy here, not knowing what's going on. And she posted those other reviews.'' He paused and Nick could practically feel his desperation through the phone. ''I'm onto something here, Nick. I've got to make this business work! I've got to!''

The sound of running water abruptly stopped, forcing Nick's gaze back to Desiree's room. ''Look, I've got to go. I'll meet you in the lobby in the morning at ten.''

''Ten?'' Ron parroted.

''Yes, ten, and not a moment before.''

''Fine. I guess that'll have to work.'' Another pause. ''The show's not over until noon. I can...I can handle it. But be prompt,'' he warned. ''That's cutting it too close for comfort.''

''Bye.'' Nick ended the call just as Desiree stepped from the shower. She smiled a greeting at him, toweled her hair. Her gaze landed on the phone at his ear and a perplexed little frown wrinkled her brow. ''Just clearing my schedule,'' Nick told her.

God, she was gorgeous. Nick couldn't imagine what had made him think her features were only passable when he first saw her. He must have been out of his mind. High on stupidity. Something. Nick took a moment to drink her in, to commit to memory the way she looked right now.

Her wet hair hung like a dark chocolate curtain, clung to her slim shoulders. Her skin, flushed from her shower, had been scrubbed clean with some sort of citrusy fragrance he could smell from here. Her

nose and cheeks were particularly shiny and that unbelievably ripe, carnal mouth he'd undoubtedly see
in his dreams from now to eternity was a luscious
natural pink, free of makeup.

Wet droplets ran down the small indentation of her
spine, over her womanly hips and heart-shaped der-
riere. She turned and Nick glimpsed the dark triangle
of curls snuggled at the apex of her thighs. Her womanly frame was firm where it should be firm and soft
where it should be soft.

She had entirely too much meat on her to be considered model perfect, but frankly Nick didn't care
for the skin-over-skeleton look that was currently so
popular. Desiree put him in mind of Marilyn Monroe.
Soft, curvy and voluptuous.

She was perfect.

"I can be ready in a few minutes," she told him
over the roar of the blow dryer.

Nick nodded. He'd heard that before, but with this
particular woman he knew better than to not believe
it. Desiree could out-multitask anyone he'd ever
known.

Fifteen minutes later, they were pulling out from
under the hotel's porte-cochere. White clouds
streaked across the clear September sky like a slash
from a painter's brush across a blue canvas. The
bright sun had already burned the dew from the
grass, promising another unseasonably warm day.

Desiree had dressed for the occasion in a red-and-
white gingham sleeveless shirt which hit her just
above her belly button, giving him a glimpse of

smooth skin above white walking shorts. She wore those sexy little sandals he loved. She'd twisted her curls up again in another claw-clip and wore a pair of designer sunglasses. Small gold hoops hung from her ears. She looked fresh and relaxed and sexy as hell.

"So, where are we headed?" Nick asked her.

"What about The High Museum of Art?" she asked. "They're featuring an Impressionist exhibition I'd like to see."

Nick nodded and aimed the car toward Midtown. The area buzzed with activity. Steel, glass and asphalt interrupted by small patches of green and the occasional tree gave the atmosphere a frenetic energy. In recent years, this particular section of Atlanta had seen tremendous growth. High-rise buildings had seemingly sprouted from the concrete overnight. Traffic was heavy for this time of morning. Pedestrians marched up and down the sidewalks as bicycles and scooters zoomed in and out between them in some sort of synchronized metropolitan dance.

Nick found a parking space several blocks away from the museum. He and Desiree joined the activity, content to stroll along, pausing every once in a while to look at things that caught her fancy. Having her small, delicate hand in his made Nick's chest swell with several foreign emotions, all of which made him feel like he could conquer the world, made him feel...happy.

He wanted to protect her, to know her every

thought. Wanted to drag her back to bed and slake his perpetual lust and then start all over again. Mostly he just *wanted*.

A blast of cool, climate-controlled air hit them the moment they walked into the impressive architectural structure of The High Museum.

"Wow," she breathed.

"Ditto," Nick seconded.

A towering atrium soared overhead, drawing the eye upward where a sleek ramp wound its way along one side. Nick and Desiree opted to take the elevator up and work their way down by way of the ramp. Each floor offered interesting displays, but nothing drew a reaction from Desiree the way the Impressionists exhibit did.

Nick had never had what one would call a keen appreciation of art, but even his untrained eye recognized the talent, the magic in these bygone artists. Degas' *Two Dancers in Blue,* Monet's *Green Reflections,* Renoir's *Madam Charpentier and Her Children* and Morisot's—one of the only women dubbed a Master from that period—*The Cradle.*

When Desiree had first mentioned going to The High, Nick hadn't been particularly thrilled, but he had to confess that he'd been pleasantly surprised and had enjoyed himself immensely. She seemed to have read as much on his face.

She lifted a brow, quirked a grin. "Liked it, did you?"

"Yeah, I did," Nick admitted.

She cast him a sidelong glance. "But you weren't expecting to."

It was a statement, not a question, but he answered anyway. He grinned, pulled the pickle off his chicken salad sandwich. They'd gone to the lower level of the museum for lunch at Alon's Bakery. "No," he told her. "I was hoping you'd want to see a Braves game."

She popped a chip in her mouth. "But now?"

"Now I'm glad you dragged me here."

"Dragged you?" She laughed, her eyes twinkling merrily. "Oh, that's rich. You tell me to pick where we go and yet you were 'dragged.' Typical male mentality, and I thought you were above it."

"You're right," Nick said after a moment. "I wasn't dragged. I was forced to come along by my gesture of selfless diplomacy."

She tugged an extra chair from another table and propped her feet up.

Nick gazed pointedly at her feet, raised an eyebrow in question.

"It's getting pretty deep in here and I don't have on my hiking boots."

He laughed out loud. "Very cute."

She batted her lashes shamelessly. "I try." She polished off another chip, took a sip of soda. "Seriously, didn't you just feel awed by the art? Moved?"

Nick nodded. Manly or not, he had.

She continued to eat her food thoughtfully. "If someone said, 'Here's the money, you've got twenty-four hours. Where do you want to go?' I'd hop a flight to Paris and spend every minute I could in the Louvre. Just soak it all in.''

Now this was an interesting tidbit. Personal, one of those rare morsels he waited for. ''Paris?''

''Definitely. Provided nothing goes wrong, I'm going there next summer to study with a master pastry chef named Pierre Roulier. He's amazing. It's a six-week course. I've been saving for a while, but—'' she hesitated, smiled ruefully ''—the tuition is steep, plus room and board, travel fees and all that.'' She shrugged. ''But that kind of training is essential in my field. More expertise, more training equals more money. It's that simple.'' She smiled again. ''So now you know what a sex-toy critic spends her money on. Exciting, huh?''

Yes, Nick thought. It was. He'd never been to Paris. Had never taken a vacation other than a three-day weekend here and there. He'd never made the time to do much of anything besides work. Nick wouldn't allow himself to wonder why he'd always put work first. Some sort of personal truth he didn't wish to unearth lay in that emotional tomb.

But the idea of going to Paris with her… Inwardly Nick smiled. Now that held appeal. That would be something Nick would make time for. Spending a vacation in the most romantic city in the world with Desiree, being swept up in her enthusiasm, sucked into the tornado of her vivacity, that would be incredible.

Nick half listened as Desiree continued to tell him

about her dreams of going to Paris, training under the renowned Pierre so-and-so. Visions of them traveling the world together kept jet-setting across his mind. There were several places he'd like to go, things he would like to do, and he couldn't help but imagine her reaction to each and every adventure.

"—and so that's why I decided to leave the convent, join the circus and become a lesbian."

Nick blinked, yanked from his thoughts. "Sorry?"

"You haven't been listening to a word I've said," she accused playfully. She propped her head against her palm. "What gives? Are my dreams boring you to death?"

"Nothing about you bores me to death," he told her, leveling his apologetic gaze on hers. "I'm sorry. I zoned out for a minute."

"I gathered that. Anything you want to share?"

No. Not yet, anyway. There were several things he needed to take care of first. Like Ron. "Oh, it was nothing really. Just—"

Her lids drooped, she faked a snore and the hand holding her head up gave way dramatically. "Oh." She blinked as though she'd just dozed off. "Sorry. What was that again?"

Nick laughed. "Point taken. Hey, I told you I was sorry. What do you want me to do?"

Without warning, her gaze dropped to his lips, lingered. "To me or for me?"

Like Lazarus from the dead, lust rose instantly. "Either," Nick managed.

She hummed under her breath. "I'll have to think

about it. But, just so you know, I have some special plans for you tonight. Don't get any ideas about blowing me off.''

That sounded promising, Nick thought, as heat pooled in his groin. ''Just so you know, I have some special plans for you as well. And you can think about blowing me off all you want.''

Her lids fluttered and she slowly licked her lips. ''I'm thinking about it,'' she told him. ''But I'd like to turn that thought into action. What do you say we go back to the hotel? I'll need a little time to prepare. My special plans come first.''

''Fine by me,'' he said quickly, eager to heed the come-hither order she'd just issued his penis. ''Let's go.''

MEG GLANCED AROUND the room one last time, made sure that everything was in order. This was her first attempt at a true seduction and she wanted everything to be as perfect as it could possibly be. Nick still needed a few lessons in Sex 101—in forfeiting control to a partner—and this would be her last night to teach him. Her last chance to show him how wonderful the unknown could sometimes be.

The thought struck a sharp pang of regret, but she forced herself not to think along those lines. She'd known when they began this week together that this would be the way things played out. She'd known...and yet that knowing had not prepared her for the keen sense of loss. Her heart squeezed painfully and moisture pricked the back of her lids.

Meg blinked, forcing the sentiment to recede. She couldn't allow herself to dwell on that now. She and Nick had precious little time left together and she didn't want to spend it mired in regret. She could weep for what might have been once she got home. Admit her true feelings for him in the privacy of her bedroom armed with a box of tissues and a gallon of ice cream, because she didn't dare admit them here, didn't dare let him suspect that what had started out as a substantial physical attraction had grown into something altogether more precious. At least, for her.

So much for a no-strings affair, Meg thought. Nick had kept the strings, unwittingly cast a net and her poor heart was hopelessly tangled up in it.

Meg pulled in a shuddering breath, summoned composure. She'd sort it out later. Right now, she just wanted to be with him. This was it, her last chance and she wanted to savor each second, relish each minute.

She'd pulled the drapes, scattered candles all around the darkened room, letting their warm glow barely illuminate the darkness. She'd sprayed the sheets with a neat little item called Sheer Satin, making the cool cotton silky to the touch. She'd loaded her bedside table with her favorite toys, favorite enhancers and a few other necessary items.

Heat rushed through her limbs at the thought of what she and Nick were about to do. What he would do to her, what she would do to him. Tonight, he would be her life-size toy, his magnificent body her playground.

Meg checked her reflection in the dresser mirror and was startled at the woman staring back at her. She wore a black-and-red silk teddy with see-through gauzy fabric over her nipples. The garment tied right between her breasts, leaving a deep inverted vee of open skin. Made of a coordinating fabric, the matching thong barely covered her mound and rode high on her hips.

Meg had taken her hair down, and the long brown waves shimmered around her almost bare shoulders. She looked like a woman ready for her man, Meg decided, pleased with the vampish ensemble. She smiled. Lot of trouble for something she couldn't wait to take off.

She knocked lightly on the connecting door. "Nick?"

He appeared almost instantly. His hot gaze roved over her body, leaving a delicious trail of warm sensation. He blinked. Swallowed. Finally, "My God."

Meg felt a cat-in-the-cream grin slide across her lips. She pirouetted. "You like?"

"Y-yes," came his strangled reply. He reached for her.

Meg slid back, beckoned him farther into the room. "Oh, no. Remember? I'm calling the shots this time…and you have to take it." She punctuated the remark with a bold caress across his groin. Nick's jaw tensed at the contact.

Meg frowned, taking in his fully clothed appearance. "To begin with, you're overdressed. Strip."

A laugh burst from his throat. "As the lady wishes."

Nick slowly began to slip his shirt buttons from their closures, revealing inch by inch the impressive form of his chest. All that smooth muscle, all that latent power, just for her. For tonight. Warmth rushed to her core. Her breasts grew heavy with want, her nipples pearled, rasping the gauzy fabric of her negligee. Her breath grew labored.

Dammit, just like that, he'd already wrested control from her. She wouldn't permit it. Not this time. Before he could painstakingly undo another button, Meg stepped forward. Her determined gaze met his knowing one. "Let me help you," she told him. "You're going to need all your strength."

Meg partially opened his shirt and, as she worked the buttons free with her fingers, pressed her lips to his chest. She found his nipple, bit lightly and sucked hard. Nick's answering groan rang with defeat, making Meg's heart soar. She learned the contours of his chest with her tongue. Listened to those little hitches in his breathing which indicated sensitive spots and committed them to memory for future use. Before her time was up, she'd make him beg. Make him lose his precious control. Make him hers.

The rogue thought had pushed its way through before she could check it.

Forcing the wish aside, she slid his shirt free of his shoulders, pushed it down his arms, then went to work on removing his pants. Meg kept constant contact with his body. She brushed her breasts against him, her hands, whatever, but never ceased that relentless touch. Kissing her way around to his back, she looped her arms around his waist, smoothed her hands down his ridged abdomen and found the button of his trousers. She pressed herself firmly against him as she slipped the button free and lowered his zipper.

His pants sagged around his waist. Meg slid her fingers under the waistband of his boxers and worked them down his hips until they joined his pants. Breathing harshly, Nick kicked the garments off his legs and out of the way. Candlelight bathed his glorious form, casting gilded shadows over his utterly male body.

His erection sprang forth, nudged his belly button. Just looking at all that virility, that part of him that made him male sent a wash of want hurtling through her.

"You're killing me," Nick growled as she gazed at him with undisguised longing.

Meg gently nudged him until he collapsed on the foot of the bed. She produced a can of whipped cream from the dresser and coated his penis in the cool, fluffy concoction. Nick hissed a breath through his teeth as she swirled it round and round, making him her own personal sundae. When she was finished, Meg set the can aside, knelt between his spread thighs, tucked her hair over her shoulder and took him in her hand. Her gaze met his as she slid her tongue slowly from the root to the tip of his hot throbbing length. A groan stuttered out of him at the contact. She licked lazily, long slow strokes of her tongue. Wrapped her lips around him—no small feat considering his enormous size—and suckled him.

Nick's thighs tensed. His hands bunched in the sheets and a low growl issued from his throat.

"That—" Meg clarified just in case he didn't understand "—is not killing you. That's torturing you. Just the way you've tortured me. Did you know I've dreamed of doing that since the first time I saw you? That I couldn't wait to taste you—" her tongue swirled around the engorged head of his penis "—here."

Another guttural sound, part growl, part cry rumbled from his chest.

She could feel the tension vibrating off him, could feel the tenuous grasp he had on his restraint barely held in check. Let it go, baby, Meg thought, taking the whole of him deep into her mouth.

She licked, sucked and massaged every hardened inch of him with the soft skin inside her mouth, with her tongue. Paid particular attention to the ultra-sensitive head, that soft, soft skin encasing his rigid arousal.

Having him in her mouth, tasting the salty evidence of his need was a singularly intoxicating experience. She loved it. Reveled in it and the knowledge made her feel all warm and mushy inside, languid. Her blood thickened, warmth drenched her feminine folds, the tiny scrap of fabric hugged against her sex.

Her mouth left off his arousal. She took him in

her hand, gently pumped him as her tongue found a new treasure. Meg laved his testicles, pulled them one at a time into her mouth and rolled them around her tongue. Nick's powerful body shuddered. He growled, and thrust impatiently against her hand.

Oh, no, Meg thought. Not yet.

She took the length of him back into her mouth and sucked him hard, in and out, in and out, squeezed his thighs, fondled him, anything she could to drive him crazy with want. She heard his sharp intake of breath. He swore. Repeatedly.

He tensed again, his thighs locked and she sensed his impending climax. Nick made a move to draw her back, but Meg forced his hand away and sucked him harder, took him deeper into her mouth, worked her tongue rhythmically along his length, until finally his entire body froze. His sweet salty seed hit the back of her throat in a rush. Meg drank him in, milked the rest of the climax from him with her lips and tongue. She cleaned him thoroughly, mewled with pleasure.

Finally, Meg placed one lingering kiss on the tip of his penis and rose from between his legs. She gazed at him, ran her tongue around her lips, showing him how much she enjoyed tasting him. "You were delicious," she purred. "Scoot back and turn over onto your stomach."

His astonished gaze met hers. "I can't believe— That was—" He blinked, astounded. "Thank you."

Meg grinned. "You're welcome. Now turn over."

Nick adamantly shook his head, reached for her

once more, his gaze feverish with want. "Please," he pleaded. "Let me touch you. Let me taste you."

Her nipples pouted and her feminine muscle tightened at his plea, but she wouldn't be swayed from her lesson. Nick had to learn that losing control every once in a while wasn't such a bad thing. She needed to remedy his tunnel vision, put things in a wider scope.

"That's not part of my special plans," Meg told him. "This is my show and I'm going to be the one doing the touching. You can touch me, taste me, when your turn rolls around."

His eyes widened and he fell back onto the bed with a frustrated sigh. A laugh stuttered out of him. "Oh, I'm going to make you pay," he promised her. "You are *so* going to pay."

Smiling, Meg scaled his incredible body, gently pushed him onto his stomach. She loved the feel of him beneath her, the power of being able to make this incredibly fashioned body quake with her touch. "And I can't wait. But for now..."

She leaned over him, snagged a small jar of Shiver Cream from the table. She loaded her finger and painted his body with it. Stars, hearts, X's, O's. From his broad shoulders, down the smooth indentation of his back, to that extraordinary ass. The very glide of her finger across something so masculine, so beautiful sent a rush of longing through her.

Nick's breath hissed out from between his teeth. "Don't tell me you've got another jar of Shi—"

Meg bent and sent a steady stream of air over his back.

Nick trembled violently. "—ver Cream."

Meg applied it everywhere she thought might draw a response from him. The backs of his knees, his ankles, the arch of his foot. She rolled him back over, sat back on her haunches and considered him thoughtfully. Painted his nipples, each rib, his belly button, a swirly trail on his inner thighs. Nick rewarded each touch of finger with a sigh, a growl, a hiss, a hum. She could listen to those little noises of pleasure forever, Meg decided.

She'd reloaded her finger and was about to apply it to his penis when Nick stayed her with his hand, his eyes widened with shock. "No, please. I—I can't take it."

Meg shrugged, slipped her fingers beneath the sheer lace over her breast and applied the pale cream to first one nipple and then the other. Nick greedily watched her every move. That melted-caramel gaze grew even more slumberous, more heavy-lidded.

"I love it when you look at me like that," she murmured, smoothing her hand down her belly. "It makes me get all muddled inside. Hot."

He smiled, one of those cocky gestures that at once annoyed and beguiled. He grasped his hardened length. "I can cure what ails you."

Oy, she was sure he could. Still… "In due time," she promised.

Meg reached across him once more, dragged her breasts across the masculine hair covering his chest.

Pleasure barbed at the contact, sent a shaft of heat straight to her moistened core. He groaned, smoothed one big hand across her rump.

Meg palmed the mini-bullet and massage glove.

He narrowed his gaze. "I don't think—"

"Good," Meg cut him off. "I don't think you should think." She slipped the bullet into the glove, tripped the switch and ran her vibrating hand over his tense abdomen.

Nick swore and his breath left him in a sigh. "Th-that's incredible."

"I'm glad you like it." Meg massaged his chest, his arms, turned his hands over and ran the pulsing glove over his palms. Watched his inhibitions melt and a smile curve those amazing lips.

She smoothed it down his legs, behind his knees, skimmed it over his hips and gradually, his inner thighs.

"I don't—"

She cupped his testicles with the glove before he could form the remainder of that protest. His semi-aroused flesh promptly swelled once again to its most impressive size.

Nick set his jaw, seemingly determined not to enjoy what his body clearly relished. Come on, Nick, Meg silently willed him. Let it go, don't deny the pleasure.

"Do you know what I'm thinking?" Meg asked him, stroking him now with the pulsating glove, working it up and down, around the tip again and again to the sound of his labored breathing.

"No," came his strangled reply.

A pearl of pleasure leaked from his tip and Meg bent down and tenderly licked the moisture away. He shuddered, groaned again. "Mmmm. I'm thinking about how wonderful it's going to be to sink down onto you, have you fill me up. Do you want me to do that, Nick?"

"Hell, yes!"

She smiled at his frantic, eyes-rolled-back-in-his-head retort, drew a condom from the bedside table and painstakingly smoothed it over the smooth hard length of him. "Then say the magic word."

"Now!"

"Close enough."

Meg abandoned the glove, removed her panties and straddled him, settling on the hard ridge of his arousal. Delight mushroomed, pushed a sigh from her lips. Her moisture coated him as he instinctively lifted his hips, slid slowly between her engorged folds, nudging the tender hood which hid her sensitive kernel of desire. Pleasure exploded inside her, little curls of heat that licked through her veins, igniting a fire only a blast of his seed would put out.

Unable to hold back any longer, she reached down and guided him into her opening, then sank slowly inch by incredible inch down until she'd fully impaled herself on him. Meg paused, squeezed her eyes shut and let the indescribable feeling of wholeness, of unparalleled bliss cascade through her. Her breath came in soft little gasps, alien to her ears and her gaze met his.

"Sweet heaven," Nick hissed, grasping her hips. Those strong fingers gripped her skin, setting off another blast of need. "You feel so good."

"So do you," Meg told him throatily, undulating her hips so that she sealed him more tightly to her. "When I'm with you, this is just about all I can think of. Having you inside me like this. Filling me up, until I don't know where you start and I begin."

Nick rocked beneath her. Slid more firmly into her heat. Rocked again. He coupled the rock with an incredible thrust, upped the tempo so that Meg's breasts danced and jiggled as he pumped in and out of her.

Harder, faster, harder.

Release built like a flame fueled by sheer sensation. Meg longed to let him take over, to let him lead her where she so very desperately wanted to go. But what could he learn from that? He still needed to learn his lesson.

With a soft cry of regret, Meg took over once more, forced him to let her set the pace. She rhythmically raised and lowered herself onto him, worked her muscles so that the intense draw and drag resistance created the most hedonistic friction between their joined bodies.

Her toes curled as a flash of light blazed behind her lids, heralding the coming of her climax. Her breath began to come in short little spurts. Her blood quickened, roared in her ears. Nick groaned, clenched his jaw and tightened his hold on her hips once more. He bucked underneath her, burying himself deeper and deeper into her. Her climax hovered just out of reach.

Almost—

Nick drove into her again and again....

Oh, yes. Almost— Please—

Ground his hips into hers. Harder now, frantic. He leaned forward and clamped his mouth on her breast. Tugged her nipple through the see-through fabric—

Meg screamed with delight as her body bowed with shock and the sweet rain of release swept her up into a maelstrom of glittering sensation. She rode out the storm, relished every wave of blessed release. A growl ripped from Nick's throat as his own orgasm blasted from his loins, bathed her womb with liquid heat. Her muscles tightened and released, tightened and released, milking him of more sensation, eddying deliciously intense aftershocks of orgasm through her sensitive mound.

A fine sheen of sweat coated their bodies. Nick still pulsed warmly inside her and Meg found herself uneager to break that special connection. She glowed from the inside out. Contentedness permeated her every cell. Breathing hard, she collapsed on top of him.

Smiling, Meg battled a hair away from her face. "That concludes...your course...on Sex 101," Meg teased. "You'll be tested...in a few minutes to see...what all you've learned. Do you...have any questions?"

A laugh bubbled up his throat. "Yeah. Is it my turn yet?"

Meg kissed his heaving chest. "Most definitely."

Incredibly, she felt him harden inside her. He ran his palms down her back, settled them over her rump. He moved inside her, small gentle thrusts that sent a whole new plethora of gratification through her. Meg purred with pleasure.

He stopped.

Perplexed, Meg lifted her head from his chest and looked into his twinkling gaze. "Do you know what time it is?" he asked casually.

Irritated, Meg undulated her hips. "Time to move your ass?"

He laughed. "Nope. It's payback time."

And for every iota of pleasure she'd given him, Nick paid her back tenfold. He teased her, tempted her, brought her to the brink and left her there again and again. He learned her with his mouth, with his hands, worshipped her with his body until she was completely wrung dry, utterly sated and left with the inherent understanding that she'd been thoroughly loved.

And one thing was abundantly clear—when in the predawn hours he finally tucked her close to his side and sleep claimed him—she would never be the same. Nick had done more than paid her back—he'd captured her heart.

Pity he hadn't even noticed.

# *14*

---

NICK AWOKE FRIDAY MORNING with a small rounded bottom pressed against his loins, a plump breast in his hand and a peculiar ache in his chest.

The bottom and breast were easily accounted for— *Desiree.*

The ache, however, was a completely different story. Nick gloomily suspected he knew its origin, but was reluctant to form the necessary coordinating thought. Because the thought made him panic, absolutely terrified him. Made him feel out of his element and out of control.

Like he'd been last night.

She'd literally blown him away. Set out to strip him of his defenses, to make him surrender to her and—terrifyingly—she'd done it. She'd systematically broken down every wall of resistance, done away with each preconceived notion regarding bed play and forced him to let someone else lead the way. Hell, even when she'd been on top of him—in the dominant position—he'd still tried to make her move to his rhythm, had still tried to set the pace.

But she hadn't let him. She'd forced him to surrender. Made him capitulate.

She'd painted him with Shiver Cream, massaged him with a vibrator—one of the toys he despised—and made him admit that he liked it. Made him beg. Nick mentally laughed. That whopping erection had been irrefutable proof that he'd enjoyed her ministrations.

Nick had thought she'd only been joking when she called their lovemaking "sex lessons," but evidently she hadn't been. True, she clearly didn't have as much experience as she might claim, but she'd recognized a flaw in his narrow-minded thinking and set about correcting it. She'd literally wanted to teach him a lesson. And she had, Nick realized, but not in the way she intended.

She'd taught him how to let someone love him.

Like she'd loved him. She'd loved him with her body, with those small capable hands, with every part of her. She'd broken him down and built him back up again. And under the weight of her selflessness, he'd finally stopped resisting her and had given in. Nick swallowed.

He supposed that's when he fell in love with her.

The thought plumbed a wellspring of emotion, happiness, sublime contentment, joy and, curiously, only a small amount of panic. He let those feelings rush through him, tested them, filed them away in The World According To Nick and when the waters of realization finally ebbed, he felt…right.

As if everything that had ever been jumbled up in his life, every loose end, had been set to rights, tied up and dealt with accordingly.

He felt right.

Now, he had to make everything right. For him, for her, and for Ron.

Ron.

Alarmed, Nick glanced at the bedside clock. Shit! He had to meet his brother in ten minutes in the lobby. A litany of curses ran through his mind as Nick gently extricated himself from the bed without waking Desiree. Though he didn't have the time, Nick paused to look at her, to drink her in.

Long chocolate curls fanned out over her bare shoulder, over her pillow. Her skin was a wash of pink over cream, simply gorgeous. Her long lashes painted shadowed crescents against her cheeks and those lips. Mercy. Even relaxed in sleep, that mouth had the power to excite him. Emotion welled in his chest, particularly tightening the area around his heart. God, she was gorgeous. Everything about her drew him, called to him on some primal level he'd never comprehend but didn't require understanding.

Nick had imagined that he'd someday fall in love, want to marry and have kids. Have the whole, "Honey, I'm home," dream. But it had always been just that. A vague fuzzy dream with only obscure shadows where his future wife and kids would be. Time hadn't been a factor. After all, he was still young, only thirty-two.

But now the dream had gelled. Come into sharp focus, and Desiree and chubby apple-cheeked little girls with chocolate curls and pouty lips had replaced the shadows. A sense of urgency had gripped him, compelled him to act now before the dream slipped away.

He was in love with her, Nick thought again, totally head over heels. If she didn't return his feelings, he'd make her just as she'd made him. Nick firmly intended to make her a permanent part of this life.

And he'd do whatever he had to do to protect her—he wouldn't let Ron ruin her.

No matter the cost.

MEG WAITED until the connecting door had closed softly behind Nick before she got up and resolutely made her way to the shower. She adjusted the tap and slid beneath the spray. Let the hot water wash away the musky scent of sex, mix with the silent tears that leaked from her lids. Emotion welled, her throat constricted and pain fisted in her chest.

It was over.

Bittersweet memories of last night flashed through her mind like a runaway projector, bringing into clear focus all they'd share and would never share again. Nick's kiss...the exquisite feel of their joined bodies...and the brilliant baptism of release.

Limited experience aside, Meg knew that what they'd shared transcended the physical—they'd connected on a spiritual level, an emotional plane that defied anything she'd ever dreamed of. At least, for her it had. Regret pricked her heart, stung her lids. Unfortunately, she didn't think that Nick shared her opinion.

Oh, he liked her, Meg knew. She didn't doubt that

at all. And there were even times last night when he'd gazed at her with so much hunger, so much torment, that she'd almost tricked herself into believing his feelings went past the physical, that he was feeling every bit of the angst and anguish associated with giving your heart to another person.

Meg managed a watery smile, recalling how he'd made love to her. He'd been tender and sweet and playful and thorough. He'd inspected every inch of her body, hadn't left a single freckle unnoted. He'd led her to climax more times than she could remember.

But he hadn't mentioned furthering their relationship, hadn't asked for her name, as he'd promised.

They'd met, had an explosive sexual relationship, the end.

And she couldn't even blame him, because that's all she'd originally planned. All she'd wanted. Just because her feelings had changed, didn't mean that the rules of this seduction had changed with them.

And she'd been the one doing the seducing. She'd decided the moment she met him that she wanted to sleep with him. Wanted to take him as her lover. Nick might have been attracted to her, but he'd held back and she'd been the one to pursue him. He'd just happened to be The One she'd been waiting for and ended up in a room next to hers.

Furthermore, Nick had never promised her anything, had never misrepresented himself at all. He'd been unfailingly honest and he deserved better than having to deal with her broken heart.

None of this was his fault—the blame lay squarely with her.

Meg turned off the shower, blew out a shaky breath. She'd come to the conclusion yesterday that if Nick didn't ask for her name last night, if he didn't show any interest in furthering their relationship, she'd leave this morning without a backward glance.

A clean break.

In the wee hours of the morning, one of those quiet moments between bouts of frenzied lovemaking, Nick had mentioned that he had an appointment at ten. Meg knew this would be her only opportunity to flee without making a total fool out of herself.

Keeping up the pretense of not having feelings for him simply wasn't in her bag of tricks, was beyond her acting ability. She knew there were women who could smile when they wanted to cry, laugh when they wanted to scream. But Meg had never mastered the artifice—she simply didn't know how to be anything other than what she felt.

And right now, she felt hopelessly miserable. She allowed herself the luxury of one good sob into her towel, then stifled the grief with determination and blew her nose. She'd cry at home. Meg was suddenly desperate for the familiar, for her house and her things. She wanted to cook, to create, to immerse herself in new recipes. But mostly she wanted to burrow, to lick her wounds in private like an injured animal.

Unfortunately right now she had to concentrate on getting out of the hotel before Nick got back. She wanted Nick to remember this week fondly, remember *her* fondly, and he wouldn't if he saw her like this, all weepy and woebegone and dejected.

This week as Desiree Moon with Nick would be a memory that she would treasure forever. Why muddy it up with a bad goodbye? Meg knew she'd never be able to form the word without crying. It would save them both a lot of grief if she simply packed quickly and left. It wouldn't take her long, after all. She'd kept everything relatively organized.

Meg dressed hurriedly, forewent makeup and pulled her hair into a loose ponytail. Urgency propelled her every action, helped stem her tears. She didn't know exactly how long Nick's meeting would last, but she didn't think he'd be gone very long. The hotel employed a noon checkout policy. She just knew she had to get out of here before she changed her mind. Before she made a fool out of herself.

Within minutes Meg had everything packed and was ready to go. She made one last sweep through the room to make absolutely certain she had everything together. She found her panties underneath the hem of the bedspread, shoved them in her purse rather than open her bag.

On impulse, she snagged a sheet of paper from the pad by the phone and scribbled one word on it for Nick. "Thanks." Meg bit her lip to keep it from trembling. She'd lay it on his bed for him to find after she'd gone.

She'd turned to go when she noticed her message light blinking. Dammit, she needed to get out of here! Meg considered leaving it, but in the end she swore again and entered the necessary code.

A slightly familiar male voice met her ears. Desperation colored his tone. "Dammit, Nick, you said you'd meet me at ten and you're not down here. Get down here *now,* big brother! Did you learn anything? Is there really an Antonio? Is she a fraud or not? I need to know. Now! I've worked something out to discredit her, but it requires your information and an encore appearance from the star critic, Desiree Moon." A loud huff then, "Hurry up!"

Meg somehow managed to replace the receiver despite her suddenly nerveless fingers. The note in her other hand crumpled in her fist, fell to the floor. She sank down onto the bed, unable to support the combined weight of her frame and Nick's betrayal. It was like college all over again....

Her heart stalled in her chest, then galloped as pain sent her pulse rocketing through her veins. Nausea welled in the back of her throat, forcing her to swallow. She'd placed the voice and within seconds translated what it meant.

Nick had come here to spy on her—to ruin her as a critic for his brother.

Ron Capshaw was his brother....

Meg swiped angrily at the tears steadily coursing down her cheeks. Everything suddenly clicked into place. Ron's peculiar attitude, Nick's tense demeanor when she'd brought up Ron's name. He hadn't been angry on her behalf as she'd so stupidly assumed— he'd been angry on his rotten brother's behalf.

Apparently Ron had suspected she'd been fabricating part of her reviews and correctly deduced her lack of experience. Quite frankly, his perceptiveness shocked her. He didn't seem smart enough to figure it out, Meg thought uncharitably.

But he had, and rather than attempt to charm her himself—when hell froze over, Meg thought with a snort—he'd asked his brother to come in and do his dirty work. Ron must have dialed her number by mistake, Meg decided. Another thought struck. She'd be willing to bet the connecting door, the whole towel set-up, everything had been orchestrated.

The bastard.

A fresh wave of tears trekked down her cheeks and a quiet sob shook her chest. Betrayal twisted like a knife in her belly, bent her double with the pain. How had she been so stupid? How had she let this happen again? She could forget Paris, forget training with Pierre. Hell, if Ron's mouth turned out to be as loud as Grant's had been, Meg would be lucky to keep her job at *Chez Renauld's*. The impact of all she'd lost and would and quite possibly lose hit Meg like a sucker punch to the gut. A soundless wail rose in her throat and she stifled it with her fist.

While she'd been falling in love, giving him her body, he'd been laughing at her, scheming how to seduce her into bed so that he could publicly embarrass her and get her fired.

And she'd made it so painfully easy for him.

Again.

Meg's face burned with humiliation. Regret and

anger boiled in her stomach when she thought of all the things she'd done to him, with him, and what she'd let him do to her. She couldn't believe she'd been so easily duped, so thoroughly deceived. Couldn't believe she'd misread his character so completely.

But she had.

Meg's lips twisted ruefully. And that's why he'd never asked for her name again. He didn't need it—she'd freely offered him the ammunition to ruin her.

The desire to curl into a ball and cry her broken heart out was almost overwhelming, but she wouldn't give Ron Capshaw or his sorry brother the satisfaction. At least, not here.

Meg stood on wobbly legs, wiped the remaining moisture from her face, summoned the tattered remnants of her pride and quickly left the room she'd shared with Nick behind. She wished she could leave everything else behind as well—like the pain, the grief, frustration and heartache, the memories—but she couldn't.

Like her broken heart, she'd carry it around with her no matter where she went.

"THANK GOD!" Ron greeted Nick desperately. "You must have gotten my message."

Nick scowled. "What message? I overslept and had a helluva time getting an elevator this close to checkout time."

Ron leaned forward anxiously. "Well? What did you find out?"

"It doesn't matter what I found out. I've come up with another sol—"

Ron's eyes widened. "What do you mean it doesn't matter?" Ron argued. "Of course it matters! What in the hell are you—"

"Would you shut up and listen?" Nick growled impatiently. "I said that I've come up with a solution. So instead of running your mouth, why don't you listen to what I have to say? That's always been your problem, Ron. Too much talk, not enough action. I know how Dad treated you was unfair, and I'm sorry that I always received so much more than what he ever gave you." Nick paused. "But that wasn't my fault, Ron. And it's time that you stopped beating me—beating Mom—over the head with it. Be a man."

Ron opened his mouth to argue, but seemingly thought better of it. He nodded.

"Now, here's what we're going to do. I'm going to level with you, be brutally honest and you probably aren't going to care for at least half of what I intend to tell you. I'm in a hurry, so listen up." Nick leveled a hard stare at his brother. "This scheme to discredit Desiree was so heinous I can't even begin to imagine how you came up with it, much less got me to participate. But you did, and I'm man enough to admit when I make a mistake. You haven't been— but you're going to be, little brother. Like Mom, I've always let you needle me into getting your way. Let guilt override my good sense." Nick's jaw firmed. "But those days are over. I know you were desperate and I can appreciate your motivation. I'll even take responsibility for my part in it. I should have had more faith in you. Should have really helped you make decisions instead of giving you money and letting you make bad ones. But this stunt has made me ashamed of you, but mostly ashamed of myself." Nick paused, swallowed as the truth of that statement hit him. "Your products suck," Nick said flatly.

Ron opened his mouth to protest, but Nick refused to let him finish.

"They suck," Nick repeated. "I tried them, tried others. Yours suck."

"That's your solution?" Ron remarked, seemingly astonished. "To tell me that my products aren't up to par?"

"No, I didn't say they weren't up to par. I said they suck. But that can be remedied. You can fix that."

Ron ground his teeth. "That takes money and in case you haven't noticed, I'm almost broke."

"That's why you need a partner."

"A partner?" Ron repeated dubiously.

"A silent partner to kick in and back you a little."

Ron snorted. "Like that'll happen when I'm about to go belly-up." He speared his hands through his hair. Defeat rounded his shoulders.

"It would if you could find someone who had faith in you. Who trusted you enough to make the improvements and helped you invest the money wisely."

"And where am I supposed to find this trusting benefactor?" Ron asked sarcastically.

Nick shrugged, managed a small smile. "You're looking at him."

Ron's eyes bugged. "What? You?"

"Sure, why not? You make the improvements and I'm confident you'll make money. Might as well make me money, too."

"Do you have that kind of cash?" Ron asked, pride and the promise of possibility drawing the slump from his shoulders.

"I can get it. I've got some things I could sell. Cash out other investments."

Ron whistled low. "Wow."

"There's only one condition," Nick told him.

"Name it," Ron breathed gratefully.

"No more money runs to Mom. Ever. Talk her into letting me invest her money. You make it, you make it." Nick shrugged. "If you don't, you start over like everyone else. Agreed?"

Ron nodded. "Agreed."

Nick extended his hand. Ron looked at the proffered hand, swallowed, then grasped Nick's outstretched palm and pumped it up and down vigorously. He smiled gratefully. "Thanks, big brother."

"You're welcome."

Pride welled in Nick's chest, glad that he and Ron had come to an agreeable solution. He didn't really know if Ron's business would fly or not, but he'd needed to give Ron the opportunity to prove himself. Their father had never done that, Nick knew. Ron had simply needed someone to have faith in him, to convince him to grow up. That's all he'd ever needed, Nick supposed, and he'd been so busy blazing his own trail, he'd never looked back and considered Ron might not have the same confidence. But he should have known that he didn't.

"We'll get together later this week and work out the details," Nick said. "I've got to get back to the room."

Ron smiled knowingly. "You like her, don't you?"

That barely scratched the surface of his feelings for Desiree, Nick thought, but nodded anyway. "Yeah. She's...special."

Ron frowned at something over Nick's shoulder. "Was she supposed to wait for you?"

"Yeah."

Ron's brow folded. "But isn't that her standing by that cab?"

Panic thundered through his veins. Nick swiveled to look over his shoulder and his eyes widened as he watched Desiree climb into a cab. Bloody hell. Nick vaulted from his chair, flew across the lobby and ran outside just as her cab taxied out from under the awning. He shouted her name, but the cab didn't slow and if she heard him, she hadn't looked back.

"Bloody hell!" he roared, startling everyone under the porte-cochere. Shaken, Nick paced back and forth, his frantic mind trying to assimilate what he'd just seen.

She'd left him. Without a backward glance. Without a goodbye.

Dammit, why would she have done that? Why hadn't she waited on him?

Something Ron had said earlier surfaced in Nick's frenzied thoughts. *You got my message.* Dread and horror ballooned inside him. If his suspicions were right...

Nick raced back inside, met his brother halfway. "You said I got your message. What message?" Nick asked.

Ron backed up a step. "I left a message this morning when you were late."

Nick blinked, forced himself to remain calm. "What did it say?"

"Just the usual stuff I've been saying all week. Get down here. Is she a fraud or not?" Ron quailed at Nick's thunderous expression. "Stuff l-like that."

Nick swore repeatedly. "Is it possible that you dialed the wrong number again?"

"I, uh—"

Overwhelmed, Nick tunneled his fingers through his hair. "Shit. Shit!" Nick pivoted and strode to the elevator. There was only one way to find out.

"I'm sorry!" Ron called to his retreating back.

Nick didn't bother to turn around, just waved an arm in dismissal. Yeah. Whatever. He should have known something like this would happen. Should have realized that he'd waited too long to make things right.

If he'd met with Ron last night instead of spending

the evening between her thighs, this wouldn't have happened. But he'd been so desperate to slake his lust—so unable to control himself—he'd ruined everything, including spending the rest of his life with her.

The realization of all he'd undoubtedly lost sucker-punched him. Emotion clogged Nick's throat and dread writhed in the pit of his belly, making him sick to his stomach.

He should have leveled with her. He should have told her the truth.

The trip down the long silent hall was the longest walk Nick had ever had to make. Because he knew she was gone, and he knew why she'd left. Resigned, Nick let himself into his room. Just as he suspected, no message light blinked from the telephone base. It had gone to hers.

Nick cursed again, collapsed onto the bed and rested his head in his hands.

She was gone.

He glanced through the connecting door she hadn't bothered to close and a dry chuckle vibrated up his throat. As usual, she'd done everything in a perfectly organized way. Not one single trace of her had been left in the room, curiously, not even the smell of her perfume.

Through this entire ordeal, Nick had been completely out of his element, so at a loss for what to do. How to make things right.

And yet, as he sat there, his chest heavy with dread, with remorse, in an empty room, Nick had never been more certain of what he needed to do in his life.

He had to find her.

He didn't know how—hell, he didn't even know her name, where she lived, had no personal details other than her career—but he had to find her. Had to explain, apologize. Make her his.

Come hell or high water, that's what he firmly intended to do.

# 15

"MEG, IT'S NICK. If you're there, please pick up. Please. Come on, I have to talk to you." Deep sigh, then. "Okay, look, I'll call back later." Dial tone.

Meg reached over and deleted the message, the same as she had every other message Nick had left on her machine since early this morning. She couldn't imagine how he'd found out her name, and quite frankly didn't understand why he'd gone to the trouble. It hadn't taken him long, only a couple of days to run her to ground.

It would seem he'd had some sort of attack of conscience, but that was too bad. If he currently wallowed in guilt, that would be his hell to deal with. She certainly didn't intend to absolve him of any of it. Between crying jags and bouts of self-loathing, Meg didn't have the strength to deal with him anymore and had begun to refer to him as just The Bastard. It was a petty comfort, but she'd take it where she could get it at this point.

Meg had arrived home with dozens of boxes in her carport, and she knew she would eventually have to get back to work. She had the money and Pierre's course to consider. But her heart simply wasn't in it.

Every time she picked up a toy, she'd think of Nick and her eyes would well with tears.

Despite everything that he'd done—the bitter betrayal—her body simply wouldn't forget him. She could force him from her mind at times, but she still craved his touch. Missed the mind-numbing release she'd only found in his traitorous arms.

The Bastard.

How screwed-up was that?

After she'd gotten home, Meg kept waiting for the other shoe to drop, for Marcus to call and fire her. But Nick's information could only hurt her if she had something to hide, so Meg had decided to call Marcus and level with him. Beat Nick to the punch. Meg had confessed about her lack of experience, confessed about Nick. Marcus had been shocked, but to her surprise, he'd said, "Well, you do a great job and it sounds like you're qualified now, doesn't it?" Surprisingly, neither Nick nor Ron had called him. And that had been that. She'd kept her job. Marcus had promised to contact Ron Capshaw and make sure that rumors didn't start to surface. This was a humiliation Meg would just as soon not share with the public at large. She'd had to tell Marcus, but she didn't plan to confide in anyone else.

Besides, knowing that he'd betrayed her didn't change her feelings for him. Regrettably, she was still in love with him. She was angry, hurt and would most likely never forgive him, but the heart only knows what the heart knows and Meg's foolish heart refused to be swayed, turning a deaf ear to reason.

In her case, the old "out of sight, out of mind" adage didn't hold true, because she hadn't been able to think about anything but Nick since she'd gotten home. While most of the thoughts had been mean-spirited, vindictive and painful, the rest had been hedonistically depraved, filled with visions of the two of them in the throes of ecstasy. If she focused really hard, she could almost feel him there, positioned between her thighs, pumping in and out of her....

Meg swore as heat rushed to her core. She had to stop this. He'd set out to seduce her, to ruin her. She shouldn't be thinking about how well he'd done it. But the initial anger and outrage had dimmed, had given way to less volatile emotions like regret and despair.

Who knew? Maybe if he hadn't been such a bastard, if he hadn't been Ron's brother and set out to seduce her and they'd met at the hotel under different circumstances, things might have worked out. The convoluted wishful thought made her laugh out loud.

Micky, her gerbil, abruptly stopped running on his wheel. He gazed at her with little black eyes and his whiskers trembled in confusion.

"Think I've gone off the deep end, do you little buddy?" Meg asked her pet. Micky ran into his soup can, clearly not up to any lengthy discussion. Just like a man, Meg snorted.

She sighed, pushed herself up from the couch and trundled into the kitchen for another ice cream anti-depressant. She'd just shoved the hot fudge into the microwave when the doorbell rang.

"Who is it?" she called through the door, not really up for company. She peered through the peephole, but something obstructed her view.

"I've got a delivery for Meg Sugarbaker. I need a signature for this one."

Meg sighed and flipped the locks. Normally they could leave packages in her carport, but she occasionally had to sign for them as well. When she opened the door, Meg immediately saw what had obstructed her view through the peephole—a huge refrigerator-sized box.

She frowned. "What is this?"

"Don't know," the deliveryman said. He tilted it on the hand-truck he'd used to maneuver it up her steps, making something heavy shift inside. Meg heard a groan and assumed the delivery guy had made it. "It's from a company called Guilty Pleasures. Where do you want it?"

"I don't— I don't know." Meg backed up a step. "I guess the living room will be fine for now."

Guilty Pleasures. Meg's mind was still reeling when the deliveryman thrust his pad under her nose for her signature. Meg hastily scribbled her name and escorted him to the door.

She turned back and thoughtfully studied the box. She couldn't imagine why Guilty Pleasures would send her anything, and furthermore, couldn't begin to guess what kind of sex toy required so much room that it would need to be packed in a refrigerator box.

Meg tentatively crossed the room and inspected

the label. The Guilty Pleasures logo, address and in big bold letters the words, BOY TOY.

Interesting, Meg thought, thoughtfully tapping her chin. Her curiosity piqued, Meg quickly went to work opening the box. One long seam lay horizontally down the front. Meg tugged the tape loose and, to her surprise, the flaps burst open.

She jumped back and screamed as packing peanuts and a naked man burst out of the box.

Nick.

Nick ducked out of the box and stood up. Other than a giant red bow tied to his genitals, and a sash reading BOY TOY draped across his chest, he was completely naked.

Flabbergasted and caught off-guard, Meg clamped a hand over her mouth, burst out laughing...until she remembered she hated him.

Nick had laughed along with her, but his chuckle had died swiftly with hers. He cast her a sheepish look. "I—"

"What the hell are you doing?" Meg shouted shrilly.

"You wouldn't answer your phone and I needed to talk to you."

Meg folded her arms over her chest, battled the renewed desire seeing him wrought. "I don't recall you being so dense. If I didn't answer my phone it's because I didn't want to talk to you."

Nick knocked a packing peanut off his foot. "I know, but I needed to explain. I needed—"

Pain made her cruel, made her want to lash out at

him. "If I would have required an explanation, I would have waited for you to come back from your meeting," Meg told him.

Nick sighed. "Meg, you've got to—"

Another thought struck. "How did you find me? How did you find out my name?"

He had the grace to look chagrined. "I went back to *The Matador*. I'd remembered you running for cover when the chef started to make his rounds." He shrugged one beautifully sculpted shoulder. "I figured he knew you."

So he had noticed. She'd wondered. "Whatever. Look, Nick, I'm sorry that you've gone to all this trouble—" she glanced pointedly at his naked body, steeled herself against it "—but, it's been for nothing. You're going to have to climb back into that box and wait for UPS to come back and get you. I should warn you, though, sometimes they can take up to a week."

Meg took supreme satisfaction in watching him quail. He looked from the box, then back to her. "Would you please just hear me out?"

She shrugged. "It's a waste of our time—particularly mine—but, sure. Go ahead and tell me why you planned to sleep with me and get me fired from my job. I'd really love to hear how you're going to justify that."

Nick met her gaze levelly and for the first time since he'd maneuvered his way into her living room, she felt perilously close to crying. "First of all, I didn't set out to seduce you, just simply get close to you, and I never said I'd try to justify it, just that I'd like to explain.''

She didn't want him to explain. He'd make her weaken, she'd throw herself at him, make a fool of herself. Meg bit her lip. Tears burned the backs of her lids. ''Go ahead. Then you leave.''

Nick blew out a breath, seemingly at a loss now that he had her undivided attention. Tension vibrated off him, shivered around him like an aura. ''Look, the long and the short of it is, I was simply trying to keep Ron from bleeding our mother dry. Ron's business was failing and he convinced me that you were the cause, that your reviews were ruining him. He thought you were a fraud and I—''

''That's ridiculous,'' Meg interrupted, outraged. ''His shoddy products were ruining his business, not my reviews.''

''I know that now, but I didn't then.'' He blew out a breath. ''Look, I'm not trying to justify what I did—I was wrong. It was sneaky and underhanded—''

''Heinous, devious and cowardly,'' Meg interjected.

Nick pushed a hand through his hair. ''That, too. And I wasn't going to seduce you. You have to believe me. I tried so hard to hold back, to not let things go so far...but I just couldn't help myself.'' Nick paused again, looking miserable. ''I want you to know that I'm very sorry. If you don't believe a word I say, please believe that. I'm truly sorry. I never meant to let things get so out of hand and then I...I just wanted to be with you.''

Meg swallowed, feeling her resolve weaken. "You mean sleep with me."

"That, too. God knows I wanted you from the moment I saw your mouth. But I mostly wanted to be with you."

Her mouth? Meg frowned with confusion.

In her distracted state, Nick moved closer to her. He tipped her chin up and ran the pad of his thumb along her bottom lip. Desire washed through her, made her reflexes sluggish. How else could she account for standing here letting him touch her?

"You have the most carnal mouth I've ever seen. It makes me hot," he murmured huskily. "Surely you don't think I was faking all that?"

No, she really hadn't. Men could fake lots of things, but an erection was hard to manufacture without the presence of need. Meg's breath hitched in her lungs. No, he'd wanted her every bit as much as she'd wanted him.

The Bastard.

She wanted him now.

"I know what I did started out for the wrong reasons, but I kept telling myself that I could fix it, if I just had more time I could make it all right." Nick paused and his tormented gaze found hers. "I did go down to see Ron, but I didn't tell him anything about you. I couldn't." Nick smiled ruefully. "I'm now a silent partner in Guilty Pleasures, the partner with the cash committed to quality products."

Meg blinked as what he'd just told her seeped like soothing glue into the broken fragments of her heart. Hope sprouted beneath her breast. "Are you say-ing—"

"I'm saying I bought into the company."

To save her job, Meg realized with a start. He'd done it for her. Joy bloomed in her chest, making a smile sneak across her lips. Unable to control herself, Meg gave into the longing to touch him and smoothed the backs of her fingers down his achingly familiar cheek.

"Will you think about forgiving me?" he asked. With a self-deprecating laugh, he gestured to his vir-tually naked body. "I'll be your Boy Toy."

Meg hummed. "Let me see," she said, slowly cir-cling him. She slid her palms down his back. Nick shuddered at her touch. "Pleasing texture."

Meg came back around and stood before him, licked his nipple, drawing another quiver from his magnificent body. "Mmmm. Wonderful taste. That's two out of three. Let's check out your size."

She gently untied the bow circling his penis and palmed him. Her lids fluttered shut as need bom-barded her. The hot, throbbing length pulsed against her palm, causing a similar sensation to commence between her thighs. Heat and moisture flooded her feminine folds. Her breasts tingled and pouted and warmth snaked through every limb. It had only been a couple of days and yet it felt like forever. "Oh, y-yeah," Meg stuttered. "Size will more than suf-fice."

Nick hissed a breath through his teeth. "So— So you'll keep me, then?"

Meg tiptoed, whispered in his ear, "That depends." She trailed her tongue down the side of his neck.

"On what?" Nick breathed.

"On whether you'll give me a free trial demonstration…right now." Smiling, Meg snagged a fluorescent condom from a nearby box and tossed it to Nick. He swiftly applied it, then groaned and kissed her.

His mouth descended hungrily to hers, the taste of him at once familiar. Wonderful. Within seconds he'd divested her of her clothes and they collapsed onto the floor. Packing peanuts stuck to her back, but Meg didn't care. She wanted him. Inside her. Now.

"Nick, you've got to—"

"I know," he growled impatiently. He clamped his lips onto her breast, sucked hard and at the same time he thrust a finger deeply inside her, testing her readiness. Meg bucked against his hand, her body quickening for the impending torrent of sensation. She kissed his neck, his shoulder, lightly bit him, desperate for the blessed weight of him between her legs. She parted her thighs, gripped his butt and eagerly met him as he plunged into her welcoming heat.

Commingled sighs of sublime satisfaction sounded in her living room as they locked together, two pieces that had come together once more to make the perfect whole. "You feel so good," he told her, raining kisses all over her face. "I've missed you."

"I've missed you, too," Meg admitted, but pillow talk came after sex, not during. She was desperate for him, utterly pathetic in her need. "Move. Your. Ass." Meg punctuated each word with a rock of her hips.

Nick chuckled. Subjected her to long, painstakingly perfect thrusts. "I think we should slow this down a little," he teased. "We've got the rest of our lives." Nick began to sing, "I love Paris in the springtime, I love Paris in the fall..."

Laughing, Meg anchored her legs around his hips, drawing him more deeply into her. "Not so fast, Slick. This is your trial run, remember?"

"Oh, well, in that case..." Nick buried himself to the hilt in her warmth, wrenching a cry of delight from Meg's throat.

"Is that...what you're...talking about?" Nick grunted, pumping harder, his big hard body pistoning in and out of her. Harder, faster, harder, pushing her further up the great mountain of release.

Meg's neck arched with pleasure and her eyes all but rolled back in her head. "Oh, yes."

"Good...I aim...to please. Satisfaction...guaranteed."

A fine coat of sweat glistened on his gorgeous form. Meg bent forward, licked the pulse point at his throat, tasting that salty essence. Tension coiled tighter and tighter inside her, spiraled hotter and hotter and pushed her further up until she finally reached the precipice and he sent her free-falling over the edge. Lights danced behind her lids, her chest heaved and the glorious aftermath of release trembled through her as her feminine muscles clenched, rode out the gusts of sensation.

With a guttural cry, Nick thrust a final time. His body arched and shuddered with the force of his climax. Breathing hard, she smoothed her hands down his back, still hungry for the feel of his skin. For him.

Nick rolled her onto her side, careful to keep himself still lodged inside her. "What…do…you say? Did I pass the free trial?"

Meg chuckled, kissed his chest. "Most definitely." She sighed. "You can be my permanent Boy Toy. I'm ready to play again. What about you?"

"Yeah, but I have a confession to make first."

Meg stilled. She'd heard that line before. "You do?"

Nick's breath stirred her hair. "Yeah…I'm in love with you."

Happiness welled, contentment saturated her every pore. "You are?"

"Unquestionably."

"Good." Meg sighed. "Wait right here. I have a gift for you."

Puzzled, Nick watched as Meg disappeared from the room. She returned in short order with something hidden behind her back.

"What are you up to?" Nick asked suspiciously.

Meg drew her hand from behind her back. A pair

of fuzzy handcuffs were fastened to one of her wrists. Sweet heaven, Nick thought. She was offering him more than her heart, she was giving him her trust as well. Something just as precious.

A tremulous smile curled her lips. "I think I'd enjoy bondage with you," she told him. "You're...special."

"Meaning?" Nick fished, lazily tugging her back down beside him. Instead of cuffing her hands together, he attached the other manacle to his own wrist, binding her to him.

Meg gazed at their joined hands. Her eyes misted with emotion, then just as quickly darkened with desire. She kissed him deeply, desperately. Nick hardened once more, quickly planted himself between her thighs and stilled, savoring the exquisite sensation of their joined bodies. Of being irrevocably linked to her. "Meaning?" Nick repeated.

"Meaning," Meg said finally, "I'm in love with you, too." She rocked her hips impatiently against him. "Now move—"

"Yeah, I know." Nick chuckled. "Move my ass."

**HARLEQUIN® Blaze™**

## GUESS WHO'S STEAMING UP THESE SHEETS...?

It's talented Blaze author Kristin Hardy!
With a hot new miniseries:

Watch for the following titles and keep an eye out for a
special bed that brings a special night to each of these
three incredible couples!

### #78 SCORING March 2003
Becka Landon and Mace Duvall know how the *game* is played,
they just can't agree on who seduced whom *first!*

### #86 AS BAD AS CAN BE May 2003
Mallory Carson and Shay O'Connor are rivals in the bar business—
but *never* in the bedroom....

### #94 SLIPPERY WHEN WET July 2003
Taylor DeWitt and Beckett Stratford *accidentally* find themselves
on the honeymoon of a lifetime!

*Don't miss this trilogy of sexy stories...*
*Available wherever Harlequin books are sold.*

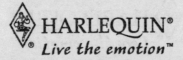

**HARLEQUIN®**
® *Live the emotion™*

**Visit us at www.eHarlequin.com**

HBBTS

*They're strong, they're sexy, they're not afraid to use
the assets Mother Nature gave them....*

Venus Messina is...

#916 **WICKED & WILLING**
by Leslie Kelly
February 2003

Sydney Colburn is...

#920 **BRAZEN & BURNING**
by Julie Elizabeth Leto
March 2003

Nicole Bennett is...

#924 **RED-HOT & RECKLESS**
by Tori Carrington
April 2003

*The Bad Girls Club...where membership has its privileges!*

**Available wherever**

**is sold....**

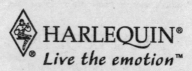

*Live the emotion*™

**Visit us at www.eHarlequin.com**

HTBGIRLS

# Pasqualie, Washington is about to see some action!

Don't miss three new linked stories
by rising star Temptation,
Duets and Blaze author Nancy Warren!

HARLEQUIN®

**HOT OFF THE PRESS**
February 2003

HARLEQUIN®

**A HICKEY FOR HARRIET
A CRADLE FOR CAROLINE**
April 2003

*Available at your favorite retail outlet.*

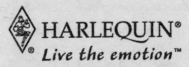

HARLEQUIN®
*Live the emotion*™

**Visit us at www.eHarlequin.com**

HDDD97NW

A "Mother of the Year" contest brings overwhelming response as thousands of women vie for the luxurious grand prize....

# Kate Hoffmann

# Jacqueline Diamond

# Jill Shalvis

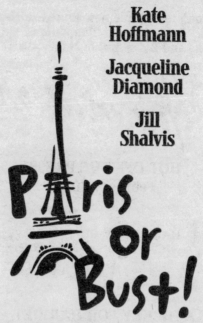

**Paris or Bust!**

A hilarious and romantic trio of new stories!

With a trip to Paris at stake, these women are determined to win! But the laughs are many as three of them discover that being finalists isn't the most excitement they'll ever have.... Falling in love is!

**Available in April 2003.**

HARLEQUIN®

*Makes any time special* ®

Visit us at www.eHarlequin.com

PHPOB

USA TODAY *bestselling author*

# JULIE
# KENNER

Brings you a supersexy tale of love and mystery…

*Silent* CONFESSIONS

A BRAND-NEW NOVEL.

Detective Jack Parker needs an education from a historical sex expert in order to crack his latest case—and bookstore owner Veronica Archer is just the person to help him. But their private lessons give Ronnie some other ideas on how the detective can help *her* sexual education….

"JULIE KENNER JUST MIGHT WELL BE THE MOST ENCHANTING AUTHOR IN TODAY'S MARKET."
—THE ROMANCE READER'S CONNECTION

*Look for*
*SILENT CONFESSIONS,*
*available in April 2003.*

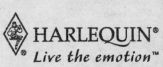

HARLEQUIN®
*Live the emotion*™

Visit us at www.eHarlequin.com

PHSC

Two women in jeopardy...
Two shattering secrets...
Two dramatic stories...

# VEILS OF DECEIT

USA TODAY bestselling author

# JASMINE CRESSWELL
## B.J. DANIELS

A riveting volume of scandalous secrets, political intrigue and unforgettable passion that you will not want to miss!

*Look for VEILS OF DECEIT in April 2003*
*at your favorite retail outlet.*

**HARLEQUIN®**
*Makes any time special* ®

Visit us at www.eHarlequin.com

PHVOD

# eHARLEQUIN.com

For great romance books at great prices,
shop www.eHarlequin.com today!

## GREAT BOOKS:
- **Extensive selection** of today's hottest
  books, including **current** releases,
  **backlist** titles and new **upcoming** books.
- **Favorite authors:** Nora Roberts,
  Debbie Macomber and more!

## GREAT DEALS:
- **Save every day:** enjoy great savings
  and special online promotions.
- *Exclusive* **online offers:** FREE books,
  bargain outlet savings, special deals.

## EASY SHOPPING:
- Easy, secure, **24-hour shopping** from the
  comfort of your own home.
- **Excerpts, reader recommendations**
  and our **Romance Legend** will help
  you choose!
- **Convenient shipping and
  payment methods.**

## Shop online
## at www.eHarlequin.com today!

INTBB2

Bestselling Harlequin Presents® author

# LYNNE GRAHAM

Brings you one of her famously
sexy Latin heroes in

## DARK ANGEL

This longer-length story is part of
the author's exciting *Sister Brides*
miniseries! Convinced the
Linwood family framed him for
embezzlement, business tycoon
Luciano de Valenza seeks
revenge against them. His plan:
to take everything that is theirs—
including their daughter, Kerry!

**Look for DARK ANGEL
in March 2003!**

HARLEQUIN®
*Makes any time special*®

Visit us at www.eHarlequin.com                    PHDA